The Partisans

Second in a Series of Novels
of the French and Indian War

Brenton C. Kemmer

FIRESIDE FICTION
2008

FIRESIDE FICTION
AN IMPRINT OF HERITAGE BOOKS, INC.

Books, CDs, and more—Worldwide

For our listing of thousands of titles see our website
at
www.HeritageBooks.com

Published 2008 by
HERITAGE BOOKS, INC.
Publishing Division
100 Railroad Ave. #104
Westminster, Maryland 21157

Other books by Brenton C. Kemmer:

Redcoats, Yankees, and Allies:
A History of Uniforms, Clothing, and Gear of the British Army
in the Lake George-Lake Champlain Corridor, 1755-1760

Freemen, Freeholders and Citizen Soldiers:
An Organizational History of Colonel Jonathan Bagley's Regiment, 1755-1760

So, Ye Want to be a Reenactor? A Living History Handbook
Brenton C. Kemmer and Karen L. Kemmer

War, Hell and Honor: A Novel of the French and Indian War

Capture and Redemption: Third in a Series of Novels of the French and Indian War

International Standard Book Numbers
Paperbound: 978-0-7884-2535-6
Clothbound: 978-0-7884-7722-5

To my lovely wife Karen and son Brenton II,
and
to our nation's many veterans,
both past and present.

Reasons and Methods

The military saga of Charles Nurse continues with this, the second in the series. I would like to take a moment and sincerely thank all of you who have enjoyed the first in the series and hope you enjoy this second volume as well. I have greatly enjoyed the comments from many of you, and especially from veterans who tell me that I have captured the true feeling of being in battle.

In this sequel, I have continued to use primary documents to not just keep the novel as historically accurate as possible, but also to assist in the dialog. I have made every effort to not make historical changes but only to interject the main characters to tell the story about the French and Indian War.

You the reader must be the true test and allow your subconscious now to slip into the 18th Century with Charles Nurse. You must allow yourself the awareness of a man of honor; a man brought up with the strict morals of old New England. You must let yourself become a man of family, a man of friends, a man who will join with his comrades and become one of *THE PARTISANS*.

Brenton C. Kemmer

BACK TO THE FRONT

The day was crisp and clear as twenty-three-year-old Charles Nurse prepared for this morning in January 1756. He had weathered the previous year's campaign on the same front as a private in Colonel Jonathan Bagley's 3rd Massachusetts Regiment. He was a tall muscular young man who had grown up working on the farm and on the wharves of Amesbury. His dark brown hair was short and coarse and his deep brown eyes were piercing at times.

Slowly he rose from his bunk and shook out his white woolen blankets. He slipped on his red waistcoat, buckled shoes and blue regimental coat and tricorn hat. He strolled past the other bunks and took his Brown Bess musket, cartridge box, haversack and canteen from the rack at the end of the bunks and walked out the barracks door. Standing there on the guard walk of the second floor of the eastern barracks building, Charles looked around the fort. The army and now the winter garrison had made great progress over the past four months raising the cribbed pine walls, building two large two-story barrack buildings and several storage buildings and a guardhouse. He slowly climbed down the stairs hoping to find a quiet spot to write a letter. He had recently returned to Fort William Henry after a short trip back to his hometown of Amesbury in the colony of Massachusetts-Bay. He had been sent with several others of the Bay colony away from their duties at Lake George to collect warm clothing that the families back home had accumulated. Charles had finished the campaign season of 1755 with his regiment and survived the Battle of Lake George, as the major fight of that past summer was beginning to be called. He had also spent some time towards the end of the season scouting with some of the different provincials from various colonies and now was preparing to jump at the chance of doing so again.

Charles walked across the parade ground and out the fort gate, passing the guard, and strolled down the path leading to the entrenched camp where his army had made its stand last summer. Then he turned west and walked several rods to a clump of trees, one of the few that still remained in the massive clearing made for the construction of the fort and for a defensive perimeter. He threw down a blanket he had been carrying over his shoulders and sat down on the frozen earth. Slowly he leaned back, resting against the tree trunk. Tilting his head up, he closed his eyes and let the sharp breeze blow across his face. The events of the past several months filled his head. He thought of the excitement of leaving home for the adventures of joining the army, the drudgery of a soldier's life, the hell of war, the fear and agony of losing friends and the voids that the time away from home had left in his heart. It had been a very eventful campaign. After a few minutes, and relaxing, Charles reached into his haversack and took out his letter book, ink and quill and began to write.

My dear Mary,

I have arrived back safely at Fort William Henry with the wagonload of warm clothing from our town. The weather had begun to take its toll on our men but our fellow Bay Colony soldiers embraced these loving articles. The men of the other colonies, especially the Yorkers, are in great need of warm clothing!

As I traversed our colony and the route from Albany to Lake George I kept myself amused remembering our quaint town of Amesbury, reminiscing the enjoyments of youth, the pleasures of my farm and work at the wharf, my friends and family, and the beauty of the Merrimac Valley during the colorful seasons.

Many are employed here continually working on the fort, the well being laid out just before I arrived. Most of our officers as well employed us in constructing crude houses for their quarters. The Colonel, Major Kingsbury and Captain Baldwin are the most recent.

One of the positive things that happened since I arrived was 187 oxen coming into our camp. Men were assigned to butcher and salt them and for the time being we have fresh beef for our rations.

I find it much different here from when I left, not just in appearance and season but also because of the reduction of soldiers to our winter garrison. The colonel worried, for shortly after I had left his officers could only account for 206 men. Now we are nearer 400, but a scant number compared to last fall.

Even though I have only been returned a short time, I have begun to experience boredom. Much of my time is spent thinking of you and my family and my visit home. I have decided to volunteer for a scout toward the French forts. It is to be lead by Captain Rogers whom I scouted with last fall. I look forward to this type of distraction, but dread the cold.

I must close this letter now as the army's dispatches are being prepared for transport to Fort Edward and onward to Albany and our letters will be sent en route with them for delivery. I hope all is well at home and await your word.

Affectionately,

Charles

Shortly after Charles handed his letter over to the courier he went to his barracks and prepared for his scouting duty. Yesterday he and several other men of the garrison received orders to draw heavy woolen greatcoats from the quartermaster's for the mission. He put it on and the wool scarf Mary had given him when he left home several weeks earlier. He put an extra shirt, woolen hose and mittens into his knapsack, grabbed his blanket roll and left his barracks. At the bottom of the steps Charles entered the commissary's office and storeroom.

"Sir, I am here to draw rations and ammunition for the six-day scout under Captain Rogers," said Charles.

"Let me see here," stated the commissary as the older, graying soldier looked down at some papers on his large desk. "Your name?"

"Charles Nurse sir, of the 3rd Massachusetts Regiment."

Several soldiers were already in the storeroom behind the desk receiving their issues. They were Thomas Greenleaf, Joseph Nichols and Gideon Lowell from Charles's regiment. Several others were there as well that Charles didn't know and in the corner stood Richard Rogers and the commissary assistant. It appeared Rogers was explaining something to the assistant as he was sorting out items and issuing them to the soldiers. Richard was a rough weather individual with fair hair and complexion.

"Hello Charles," greeted Thomas.

"Morning Tom," answered Charles. Then he nodded and added, "Joseph, Gideon." The two men returned the nod. Joseph had moved to Amesbury from Haverhill in 1743 and had taken up work at the local wheelwright shop. He had only a basic education, but a deep patriot drive that impressed may men his senior. Thomas was middle aged and had grown up in Amesbury, worked on the wharf with Charles and his father Caleb Nurse. They were family friends and Thomas's wife was a friend of Charles's mother, Martha, and was one of the town's midwives.

The commissary interrupted, "Nurse, here you are, six day scout, Captain Rogers, rations and 60 rounds for your musket, skates and snowshoes, complete." He tore off a receipt and handed it to Charles. "Give this to the sergeant over there," and he pointed to the commissary assistant without looking up.

Charles walked over to the sergeant and he and Richard Rogers both stopped talking and looked up at him.

"Nurse, I see you're ready to venture out with us again huh?" grinned Rogers. "You didn't get enough of us or those Frenchmen yet?"

The sergeant reached forward, "Let's see your receipt."

Charles handed it to him and smiled at Rogers and replied, "I was sent back home for warm winter clothing for our men last month and I almost thought about staying there, but then again I didn't want to leave unfinished business out here so far away from home, so I figured I'd go a scout'en to break up the monotony around here."

"Get your rations and fall out on the parade ground then," answered Rogers as he shook his head.

"Here you are Nurse," said the sergeant, as he handed things to Charles. "Three pounds of salt beef, three of hard bread, a pound of cheese." Charles placed this in his haversack. "Four gill of rum." Charles opened his canteen and the sergeant ladled the rum slowly from a keg into the canteen. "Sixty rounds for your musket. Do you want rolled rounds or loose powder and ball?"

"Cartridges," replied Charles as he opened his cartridge box and began filling it.

Just then Captains Symes, Burk and George walked in the door. The commissary laid his glasses on the table and inquired, "Yes gentlemen, what can I help you with?"

Burk answered, "Just seeing that the rest of the men are almost ready, carry on."

William Symes stood about five foot ten and was a stocky man. He had captained a New Hampshire company and had volunteered to stay on this winter. John Burk and Samuel George had volunteered when Charles had, back in the spring of '55. Samuel had been promoted to an officer after the Battle of Lake George. Burk had been the captain through the last campaign. The three had known each other as neighbors back home in Amesbury.

After Charles was finished, he walked out onto the parade to join the men already forming up. A light shower was falling now and Charles pulled his scarf tighter around his neck. Sergeant John McCurdy was giving orders.

"Fall in goddammit! Make sure you have all your gear! Captain Rogers aint gonna wait for no one!" He was a bull of a man, short with a thick neck like a buck in rut. His face had stubble from not shaving for several days and his eyebrows were bold and un-separated. He had volunteered to stay the winter with Rogers serving as his sergeant.

Charles stepped into the line of men. The three officers were standing out front of the troops talking to several other officers with their backs to the forming soldiers. Since the men in line were still talking, Charles introduced himself to the men on each side of himself.

"I'm Charles Nurse of Massachusetts."

"Thomas Cunningham, New Hampshire."

"James McNeil, corporal from Blanchard's old ranging company. Still fighten for the Captain," McNeil exclaimed.

Before anyone else could say much else Richard Rogers walked up to the formation and bellowed, "Take Care!"

The two officers out front turned around. The one on the right Charles recognized immediately. It was Robert Rogers. There was no way of missing his stern, prominent features. He had the warn features of a veteran frontiersman. Rogers was tall, around six feet, and his pronounced eyes and nose were dominant in his appearance.

The rest of the officers stood tall and Captain Rogers took several strides forward and began pacing up and down the line of men giving orders. His eyes darted over their gear, not to miss any voids, and his slight Scotch-Irish accent was low and gravely.

"Men you have volunteered for a scouting party. I see you have all prepared yourselves for the cold." He looked up at the sky and added, "and now we must include wet and cold. There are seventeen of us including myself. Captains Symes, Burk and George will accompany us. You all know my lieutenant Richard Rogers and my other officer ensign Noah Johnson." Rogers pointed to them as he named them. Johnson was an average built man who had been a farmer in Dunstable, New Hampshire. He had join Blanchard's Regiment in '55 and was Rogers' sergeant during last year's campaign. Now he was serving as his junior officer.

"We are proceeding on skates along the lake. Our mission is to reconnoiter the French forts and try and capture some prisoners. Any questions?" He paused. There was silence. "Alright then, Sergeant, get them down to the lake so we can head out."

"Yes sir," replied McCurdy. "Follow me!"

The soldiers instantly followed the sergeant and Charles noticed Colonel Bagley had walked up and was talking to Rogers and the other officers who followed shortly. Bagley was a tall, dignified gentleman of thirty-nine who before the war owned property, a wharf and had captained his own ship to the West Indies. He had served as the regiment's lieutenant colonel until the colonel, Moses Titcomb, was killed in the Battle of Lake George. At the end of the campaign he was promoted to the colonelcy of the regiment and placed as commandant of both the Fort William Henry and Fort Edward garrisons.

At the waterfront Charles and the others knelt down and tied on their skates. Then Rogers and the other officers joined the party. Rogers put on his skates, and, standing up, gave his orders. "Single file, keep up, quiet on the march, keep out away from shore. Lieutenant, you have the rear guard." He then slung his musket over his right shoulder and stepped off onto the ice and began to glide forward down the lake followed by the entire detachment.

The light rain had started to melt the skim of snow on the lake making the ice a fast silvery mirror.   Charles quickly gained a rhythmic momentum and before they realized it they were amongst the many small islands near Tongue Mountain.   It was midday and Rogers raised a hand aloft signaling a stop.   Quickly the detachment followed him onto an island so they could sit and relax in the shelter of some cedars.

After a short rest they were off again, skating up the lake.   Shortly before dusk Charles could see a small peninsula jetting out from the western shore and within minutes Rogers veered the scouting party toward it.   Again the men left the ice of Lake George for the shelter of the forest.

"Stay together in groups of four.   Two at watch at all times while the others eat and sleep.   Symes, Burk, Richard with me.   George you have the main party.   We'll be back shortly," ordered Rogers.

The three officers scurried into the woods with Rogers and the rest broke off into three groups and found a spot to rest.   Charles, Thomas Greenleaf, Joseph Nichols and Gideon Lowell stepped over to a fallen clump of cedars.   This uprooting was fresh and the massive root ball created a wind block for the men.   Charles and Thomas sat on a fallen log, Joseph stood looking into the woods and Gideon crouched down, cradling his musket in his arms facing the trail they had just left off the lake.   Gideon was a friend from home who had join up with the other men of Amesbury in '55 and served as a corporal.   He had worked at his family's wharf.

"It's been a few years since I've been on skates like this. I'm exhausted," exclaimed Charles.

"When I was a lad, we would skate down the Pow Wow to the Merrimac and see if we could make it to the coast.   Didn't make it but once though," replied Thomas.

Both men removed some rations from their haversacks and ate a cold meal and then traded with the other two so they could eat as well.   In less than forty-five minutes Rogers and the others were back.   He posted sentries and ordered all others to get some sleep.   Charles had no problem.   He fell asleep almost instantly.

Shortly before six a.m. Rogers came around waking all those who were not on guard.   They ate a quick meal of cold bread and salt beef and were back on the lake once more.   The weather was fair and column, which refreshed the men's spirits.

Some time around noon they could see a large bald-faced mountain on the western shore.   Rogers let the men, one by one, skate past him and he told them all to keep very close to shore.   A little distance past the mountain the lake began narrowing and just before dusk Charles could hear faint sounds of rushing water from the falls at the very head of Lake George. Rogers motioned for the party to turn to the east and they exited the lake and removed their skates. Moving inland about a half mile Rogers stopped the column and gave orders.

"Richard, Archibald, Henry, McNeil you have the first watch. The rest of you split up into three groups, but keep within two rods from each other group. Rotate guards every half hour. Wrap up and keep your heat in."

The men again split off into small groups and each man untied his blanket and pulled it tight around his shoulders. It had been a strenuous two days and most of the men slept for several hours.

Corporal McNeil awakened Charles. "Wake up, you rascals," he said in a soft Irish accent as he walked amongst the men, shaking them if they did not move. "The captain wants to move on, let's go." McNeil was a hot-tempered, redheaded man who had proven himself in Rogers' corps.

Rogers then sent forward Sergeant McCurdy and Private Cunningham to see if there were any signs of the enemy to the west. Returning shortly with no sign, Rogers ordered his brother to take the rear guard, placed Noah Johnson on the left flank and Jonathan Noyes on the right. Rogers himself took the forward position and everyone else followed him single file. Going was rough, finding their footing in the dark by a partial moon. Slowly they marched, stepping one by one in each other's footprints.

After about four hours the captain halted the men and sent Sergeant McCurdy forward to reconnoiter. When he returned, he reported that Wood Creek was just a few hundred yards before them and he saw no sign of the enemy on the water. They made it down to the water's edge and Rogers told the party, "I want a single rank, six paces apart, and once we hit the ice we will make haste straight across in that fashion. That way if we're spotted they cannot tell our number. Form up and march."

The men strung themselves out as ordered, Rogers gave a gesture with his arm and they all rushed quickly across the creek. Once in the cover of the woods again Rogers reformed the unit and they marched north along the creek up the east shore of Lake Champlain. Being a clear night they could just make out periodically a flickering of a lantern at Fort Carillon on the west shore. About four a.m. they halted on a small peninsula. Rogers pulled the party all together.

"This is our destination. I want all of you to take time and conceal yourself on the water's edge of this peninsula. I expect some enemy parties to pass near in the morning traveling between the enemy forts. I intend to attack a party and take prisoners. Johnson, you take McNeil and Henry and find a spot fifty rods back down the lake to hide. If the enemy gets past us you stop them. The rest of us, no firing unless I fire or you're fired on. If it's a small enough party we will try and take them without firing. Take positions and wait.

A soft golden glow began to rise from the east. It slowly hit the mountains in the distant west and worked its way back toward the east as it skimmed the treetops. Charles was hunkered down in a thicket right on the water's edge. Beside him sat Thomas Cunningham, Joseph Nichols and Jonathan Noyes. Cunningham was fidgeting with the flint in his musket. All four were facing different directions so as not to be surprised by the enemy. Charles was facing up the lake. It was hard for his eyes to focus long in the distance because of the cool morning breeze and his lack of sleep. Then a movement caught his eye. A horse-drawn sledge came into his view. He reached around behind his back and placed his hand on Cunningham's shoulder. Cunningham closed the pan on his musket and Charles gestured that there was movement on the lake before him. The four men now had adjusted their positions and were preparing to explode onto the ice or fire a volley on Captain Rogers' orders. Then a second sledge came into view. Within moments the first sledge was almost before them.

Suddenly, from the bushes to the right, Rogers, his brother Richard, McCurdy and Symes busted out onto the ice and made a dash for the sledge. Charles and the men with him hit the ice right on their heels. The horse pulling the first sledge reared and the driver snapped the reins and they lurched forward. The second sledge, seeing men on the ice, quickly turned about and dashed back up the lake. Symes and Richard Rogers jumped in front of the horse's path. The man setting beside the driver began to pull up to aim his musket at the two men in front of them and Captain Rogers and McCurdy leaped into the sledge. Rogers knocked the man who was wielding the musket to the ground and McCurdy jumped on the other, wrestling the reins from him and bringing the sledge to a stop. By this time Charles and the others had reached the sledge. A third party lead by Samuel George was sprinting toward the retreating second sledge. Rogers grabbed his prisoner and threw him on the ice in front of Charles. "Nurse, tie his hands and keep him with you."

Charles pulled a thong from his haversack and bound the man as ordered. The others in his party grabbed the horse. Rogers turned immediately to see where the second sledge was. By this time the retreating sledge had made great headway and the chasing men had turned around and were coming back toward the ambush spot. Surveying the area quickly Rogers started to give orders.

"Nurse, McCurdy keep those prisoners separate and gag them. Make sure they are searched. Cunningham, get over to Ensign Johnson's ambush spot and have them fall back into the woods and keep their eyes open. We'll be joining them quickly. Richard what's in that sledge?"

Richard lifted the canvas and stated, "Beef, fresh beef."

"Get those prisoners in the woods," Rogers further ordered. Then he turned to Symes and said, "We can't take this beef and we can't leave it here or let the horse go. Knock the horse in the head and the rest of you start chopping away the ice all around the horse and sledge. Let's get them into the ice and get on our way before we're spotted."

Samuel George and his party had now returned and Rogers gave him orders, "George, take your men into the woods and set up a perimeter until we join you."

Within minutes the evidence that the sledge and that Rogers' party had been in the area had been sunk and all had joined together once more in the woods on the west shore. Rogers then issued orders.

"McCurdy and I will take point. Ensign Johnson, you take McNeil with you as rear guard. Captain Symes you and Archibald have the right flank and Richard, you and Henry take the left. Nurse and Cunningham, you have the prisoners. Keep them separated and quiet. Knock 'em in the head if you need to. The rest of you keep single file and everyone keep your eyes open. We need to move quick. Change the prime in your pans. Let's move out."

The party wasted no time and traversed the east shore of Lake Champlain, reaching into the South Bay area. The weather was pleasant and made the travel through the woods easy. It also would make it easy for the enemy to spot them so they were very cautious. By sunset they had made it to a large island and Rogers motioned all to cross the bay and take up positions for a rest. Then after about three hours he ordered McCurdy and Richard to go out and make sure the area was clear. When they returned they reported that they had found no sign of the enemy so Rogers ordered them to put on their skates and they were off again. This made for a much faster travel and they slid down the rest of South Bay. By sunrise it had started to snow and within two hours they had reached the end of South Bay and took a quick break as they removed their skates and took some well-needed nourishment. The snow was coming down now so heavy they could only see about fifty yards before them. Then they were off again, this time across country toward the west and Lake George. Charles this time had the point with Rogers.

"If it keeps up like this we may have a hard time of making it in today," offered Charles.

"We are more than halfway home now. As long as we don't run into any enemy parties or Indians we should make it," replied Rogers. "You should be used to this, you're from Amesbury, aren't you?"

"Yes, born and raised. I haven't had many times when I've had to travel on foot the distance that we are covering in this snow though. This is a real challenge," said Charles.

The men started to breathe heavier from the exertion and the heavy wind in their faces. Within an hour Rogers halted the party again.

"The snow is too deep. Pass the word to put on the snowshoes, otherwise we'll not make it to the fort until tomorrow," Rogers ordered Burk, who was in charge of the main party.

About two hours later they had made it to Lake George and Rogers led the party onto the lake. They were in the area of the islands so all were keeping an eye open for hidden enemy. Shortly after dusk they reached the bay where the fort rested. About a half hour later, it must have been about 6:30, Rogers pointed his musket into the air and fired it. Almost immediately a musket was fired from about two hundred yards before them and drums started to beat. They had arrived back at Fort William Henry and Rogers' gunshot must have alarmed the camp.

Soon they could see the fort nestled atop its knoll.

"Who goes there?" shouted a voice from a group of men from the shore who had been dispatched to investigate.

"Rogers!" came the answer.

"Come on in, Sir," replied the guard.

The men marched onto the beach, up the small hill and around into the fort's gate. At the parade ground Sergeant McCurdy formed the men one last time.

"Fall in," he ordered.

Rogers stepped up in front of the detachment and spoke.

"Good job, men. Get some dry clothes on and something warm in your stomachs. Sergeant, make sure if any of the men have ailments from the weather that they report to one of the surgeons. Have the prisoners confined and keep them separate. I'll be reporting to Colonel Bagley and then be right over to question the prisoners. Get someone there who knows French. Dismiss the men."

McCurdy snapped a quick salute and Rogers returned it. Then Rogers strode across the parade ground to the colonel's office and McCurdy dismissed the men. All needed a good rest.

A COVERT EFFORT

For the next three weeks Charles performed various duties at Fort William Henry. He used his carpentry skills within the fort, contributed his strong back toward making improvements on the entrenched camp area from the previous year, and helped with a lot of clerical duties for the garrison. Although he missed the adventure of scouting with the others from the regiment, he welcomed the chance to stay out of the winter elements. This is not to say that he had not kept up on events from the scouts that were still venturing out. Charles was becoming quite good friends with some of the men from New Hampshire, and their stories filled many evenings when they would return to the barracks for their short breaks.

The end of February was drawing near. The weather had been very cold for almost a week and Charles was eager to break the monotony of daily garrison life. Hearing news of the formation of a large scout, he requested that Captain Rogers add him to his roster of men for the expedition. Rogers agreed, as long as Charles would come prepared to keep records and make drawings if necessary.

Charles climbed down from his bunk early in the morning on the 29th. He knelt down and rekindled the fire in the fireplace at the end of the barracks room, and placed the tin mess kettle on the coals to reheat last night's meal. Then he filled his tin mug from the barrel of water that sat by the fire. He placed the mug also in the fire to heat. Then he took his time dressing in his heaviest woolens, preparing himself for the scout. When he was dressed he took his mug from the coals. Placing it on the table he took out his soldier's knife and shaved some chocolate into the hot water and added some sugar from a pouch. Then he took some paper and his quill and inkpot from his haversack and sat on the bench at the table. He sipped his drink and began to write a letter to his parents.

My dear Mother and Father,

Since I have talked to you last I have been busy here at Fort William Henry. This morn I am preparing with many others for a long scout to the north.

The weather has been very cold and the garrison has suffered some, especially the Yorkers. They do not have enough winter clothing and they are even in want of blankets. Their colony for some reason has not seen fit to attend to their needs. The snow deeper than we are accustomed to in the Bay Colony. Occasionally, tall drifts build up against the fort's walls. We have had some storms bringing more than a foot of snow, with strong winds like those off the coast of our colony. More warm clothing was delivered to us recently from the good people back home. The poor men of New York stood and glared as we joyfully unloaded our bounty.

Rations are becoming scarce for everyone here in garrison. Many of our staples are running dangerously low and at times this take its toll on our bodies and minds. We have not had bread for ten days now!

I have spent many days doing carpentry on the finish work of the buildings. The barracks are livable and make a nice arrangement over the alternative, tents. I have worked quite extensively on several officers' houses. These are definitely not as extravagant as our homes back in Amesbury, but some are palaces compared to our barrack. The colonel's house has four rooms. There is an orderly room and reception room downstairs and an office and bedchamber above. The heat from his iron woodstoves puts off much more heat than fireplaces do.

We had an interesting pleasure the other day. The entire garrison went out and fired at marks. At times it became a contest, especially among the rangers. One of the most competitive was Captain Rogers. His reputation grows daily. A package was delivered to him this past week from a group of officers from Albany. They had taken a collection and purchased him a fine suit of gray, woolen broadcloth. What a change from his usual woods clothes. Also, within his package were sixteen pounds for the pleasure of his men. He was kind enough to invite me to take some madera, cheese and bread with them, since I have accompanied them on several missions.

Time is dwindling and I must leave my writing and finish preparing for our march. We are to leave today within the hour. I will have this letter sent on the next post to Albany. Hope all is going well back home. Give my best to my brothers, our neighbors and Mary and her mother.

Your loving son,
Charles

Charles packed some heavy woolen hose, an extra woolen shirt and some heavy wool lined moccasins in his knapsack. Then, donning his heavy, brown woolen greatcoat, he strapped on his pouches and belt and took up his musket and climbed down the barrack stairs. There were men forming on the parade already. He quickly joined them. Along with Thomas Greenleaf, Joseph Nichols and Gideon Lowell, there were around fifty others, most appearing to be the Hampshire men who were part of Rogers' company. Out front of the assemblage was a group of officers obviously joining the expedition. Charles knew most of them by sight. There were Colonel Glasier and Jeduthan Baldwin of Massachusetts, Captain Israel Putnam of Connecticut, Captain Parker Smith and, of course, Captain Rogers.

"Check your prime," ordered Noah Johnson, Rogers' Ensign.

"Make sure you have everything ordered by the captain," bellowed Sergeant McCurdy. He spat on the ground before himself. "This will be no stroll." As he looked up to the sky and pulled his scarf closer around his neck, he continued. "We're in for a real cold one this time." Glancing over at James McNeil, he ordered, "Corporal, form the men for the march, single file. Keep 'em spread out so one ball won't go through too many at once. Form!"

Rogers and Putnam marched toward the fort gate. As he passed McNeil Rogers ordered, "Let's move, Corporal. I have the point."

The corporal quickly issued orders and moved the party out the fort gate. "All right you riff-raff! Johnson, you and Silaway, Waldleigh and Kiser take the rear guard. Mr. Smith and his men will take the left flank. Mr. Baldwin and his Massachusetts men, take the right. The rest, single file, and keep three paces apart. To the front, march."

As soon as they had cleared the gate, Baldwin took Charles, Greenleaf, Nichols and Lowell to just inside the water's edge and centered his squad on the main column. Rogers and Putnam had reached the tree line. Rogers motioned over his shoulder for the party to follow him, and everyone disappeared into the forest.

The going was rough, for the snow was knee-deep. Fortunately for the main party, they were on the Indian trail leading north down the lake. After a short distance, Baldwin stopped his men and had them put on their snowshoes, as they were breaking trail without a path. The wind blew hard and made the cold bite at their faces as it snapped like a cat-o'-nine tails off the lake.

Late in the afternoon, they reached a creek just over halfway to the second narrows. Ahead, Rogers and Putnam crouched down in the snow and Rogers motioned for the men to do the same. He sent Putnam back with orders for a small party to come up by him. Rogers advanced cautiously with the few men. Before them was a small-entrenched redoubt and a small Indian trade town. After he was sure it was safe, he ordered Putnam to lead the men forward. The men dispersed into small groups, hunkering around the trees and the log redoubt. Guards were posted, and they took food from their haversacks and ate, and refreshed themselves from their canteens. There were a few men that were having a very hard time of keeping up. Rogers called Sergeant Archibald over to him and gave him orders to take back to camp the men who were suffering. "They have become ill. I cannot afford to have them slow us down. Make sure you do not draw attention to your group with fires. There are five men I put under your care. See to it you get them back to the fort by noon tomorrow."

Then they were off again, minus Archibald and the five men.

A short distance on their march the Massachusetts men saw a movement before them near the lake. Baldwin immediately halted his men and motioned for the column to stop. All the men on the right flanking party strained their eyes toward the wooded shore. Their hearts raced and they slowly brought their muskets to a ready position. Then from the trees burst a deer with a large wolf on his heels. The buck snorted in fright as he sprinted toward the lake to gain his safety. The wolf, with great rhythmic strides, was about to pounce on the deer's hindquarters when the deer dropped from sight and threw itself down the bank into the lake. The light crust of ice could not bear his weight and he broke through and began to swim across the lake. The wolf stopped at the edge of the bank and put his head down as if to scowl at the deer. Then, raising his head, he caught the smell of humans and sped back into the forest. The men regained their composure and the column was motioned on.

It was nearing dusk when Rogers and Putnam reached North West Bay. They skirted it to the base of Tongue Mountain. Here the party was halted and the NCOs and officers were called together for Rogers' orders. "I want to secure an area of about twenty-five rods. We cannot afford any fires, so have your men use everything they have to keep warm. Keep them close together. I want four guards and two roaming guards at all times. Have half the men on watch and the other half resting. Now see to your men."

It was an extremely bitter cold night for the soldiers. Most could not sleep but huddled together, sharing blankets, shivering, trying to conserve some body heat.

At sunrise the sergeants and corporals roused the men, though most were not asleep. They began their march again. Traveling north, their first obstacle was over a large mountain called Parker's Mountain. The wind had slowed, which eased some of their distress. They must have only made about ten miles that day, as the terrain was much hillier. By dusk, the party had reached a low area. Rogers stopped the column. By now the men were becoming quite exhausted. Rogers gave orders.

"We can not risk fires and I know you are cold and tired. Half of you need to remain on watch but the rest of you must sleep tonight. Cut hemlock boughs for bedding and make some lean-tos of sticks and boughs. This will make the cold more bearable tonight."

The men who were not placed on guard broke off into small parties and began to collect what they would need. Charles, Thomas, Joseph, Gideon, William Cunningham and Nathaniel Smith did as ordered. They cut boughs and collected sticks for a small shelter. They placed several Y-shaped sticks in the snow between two trees and laid a cross piece over the uprights. Then they propped up some other sticks and began piling up boughs on the lean-to. Finally, the men piled boughs two feet thick for a mattress to sleep on. Then they laid down two blankets and crawled into the lean-to and covered themselves with their remaining blankets.

"Not like at home, but it will do, won't it, Nurse," chuckled William.

"It's not like my featherbed, but I'm willing to give it a try. It almost feels like heaven!" sighed Charles.

The men fared much better that night and most were able to get a deserved rest.

At sunrise they were off marching in a northwesterly direction toward a mountain range. Charles and his group of Massachusetts men were put on the rear guard this time as they climbed over the peaks. Nearing noon they halted and took a rest. Charles ate dried beef and bread.

Off to the north, the men could see gray-blue clouds rolling toward them. The temperature dropped slightly and within minutes it began to snow. Luckily, the wind did not pick up, but with the temperature being somewhat moderate, the snow was very wet. Rogers gave the order and they moved onward, this time toward the north by northeast.

The travel became very laborsome, as they were slipping and sliding through the woods. The snow became heavy and the men were also becoming quite wet. At times when they were descending mountains, they were forced to sit and slide to the valleys. The extra tension on their muscles and the extreme efforts were very exhausting. Finally, near sunset they stopped for the evening. The snow had fallen nearly an inch an hour. Putting on what dry clothes they had brought, they brushed out niches in the snow and wrapped themselves in blankets to weather another frosty evening.

The men were becoming tired now, and the travel and weather were beginning to take a toll. Beginning as usual, they awoke before sunrise and began their march early. With the slippery snow of the day before and their worn bodies, they were barely able to march eleven miles to the northeast that day.

It was extremely difficult for the sergeants and corporals to rouse and motivate the men the next day. Slowly they progressed until about eleven in the morning. The column was stopped and Sergeant

McNeil was sent back to have the men come up slowly. Lying on a ridge in front of them as they came forward were Rogers, Putnam and the men who had made up the right guard. Rogers motioned the men forward and Charles and the others of the main body slowly inched forward and took up prone positions along the ridge. Charles was beside Captain Putnam.

"Peer off there as far as you can, lad," Putnam pointed. "See that tiny point of land there that juts out slightly into the lake, up by where it narrows? That's where the papists' fort is, Fort Sainte Frederic they call it. Don't want to be seen, so we'll be keepin' very alert from here on in."

Charles stretched forward and could see the point of land that Putnam was showing him. He could just make out a little bit of white on the very point, which he thought must be the French fort.

Rogers and Putnam slowly started backing down off the ridge and motioned for the men to follow them. They reformed and began to march around the ridge. Once out of sight of the fort, Rogers stopped them again. From his vantage in the front of the column, Charles could see Rogers and Putnam talking. Rogers pulled a compass from his haversack and held it in the palm of his hand and pointed in front of him, which was north. They then headed out again. Snow began to fall once again, but this time it was important to cover their tracks, being so close to the forts. After about eight miles the party stopped. Rogers pointed to his right and Captain Putnam motioned for his Connecticut men to follow him, and he took the lead. Rogers came back into the main column and they were off again. Nearing dusk, Putnam sent back one of his men and Rogers quickly moved forward. Then all but two returned to the column. One of the men had the other officers and Captain Baldwin move up with the Massachusetts men. Moving up, they could see Rogers, Putnam and the two Connecticut men looking from behind some trees on the edge of a small mountain. Rogers motioned for them to join them. Slowly the officers, Thomas, Charles, Gideon and Joseph moved up to the tree edge.

In a very gravelly soft voice Rogers spoke to them. "Down there. See, that's the French fort. We're going to wait here tonight in sight of it until the moon goes behind the clouds. I want to see if we can't cross the lake. We need to get to the other side. I believe it would be in our general interest to lay an ambush on the road on the east side. Baldwin, you and your men are going to have the first watch. Under no circumstances are you to fire your weapons unless you are fired on first. If you see movement coming toward you, send a runner back to the main party. Stay undercover here. Half on duty half off all night. You are not to leave your duty. No fires and no smoking, we're too close, they will smell us." Then he and the others slipped back into the woods.

Baldwin then whispered his orders. "Nurse, you and Greenleaf have the first watch. No talking, and pay attention to Captain Rogers' orders. The rest of us will get some food and sleep. Wake me up in four hours and I'll relieve you."

The other men took their time and ate some rations from their haversacks, and then tried to sleep. It was a moonlit night and Charles could see clearly. The moon shone off the windswept ice near the point, and the drifts along the lake's edge looked like rolls of carded wool from his mother's spinning basket. On the point Charles could make out the ramparts of the fort. They appeared to be in the shape of a star. Their stone walls shone white in the moonlight. He could barely make out a set of inner works as well. In the center of the fort stood a small castle-like tower of stone. It was a slender structure and looked as if it were at least four stories tall, like the height of Faneuil Hall back in Boston. There were four large chimneys reaching out of its roof and atop it stood the white French flag. Peering very long at the structure, Charles thought he could see many cannon in the windows of the castle. From his vantage he thought he could count at least twenty in the tower alone!

Charles shivered and pulled his greatcoat tighter over his shoulders, and wrapped his scarf across his nose and mouth. When the finely woven scarf touched his face he was reminded of Mary and her touch when he left home last, and how he had bent forward and she had wrapped it around his neck. He also remembered her reassurances to him, and how he pledged to return. He sat half the evening watching the fort, wondering about his parents, brothers, Mary and the others that he had left behind. He would return again, but in the meantime his current responsibilities were most important. Around eleven he gently woke Captain Baldwin, and he and Thomas were relieved for their turn at getting some sleep. The clouds had started to move in and cover some of the moonlight.

Around two in the morning everyone was awakened. The moon was clouded over and it was time to try and cross the lake. Rogers took the lead, skirting quietly along the steep bank of the lake. It was slippery and everyone was very careful of his footing. Then from the front of the column there was a rustling and a crash from the ice below. All knelt down and peered over the bank, twenty-five feet to the ice below. Rogers had slipped on some hidden rocks and plunged over the edge. The ice had easily broken from his weight, and he now was desperately trying to make it onto stable ice or to grab hold of something on the steep bank to pull himself from the frigid waters. The weight of his wet clothing, gear and musket were adding to his difficulties but he didn't dare release his weapon or belongings to the lake. Noon could make it down the bank to help him. McNeil and Putnam ran forward, hoping to find a path down to the water, but to no avail. Finally, Rogers was able to latch onto a strong root on the bank, and pulled himself from the water. Then, by quickly lashing belts and clothing together, several men lowered a line to the captain. Holding on tightly, he was lifted up the bank as he used every conceivable foothold he could find. The unit rushed back into the forest and Rogers stripped off his wet clothing and put on dry things that the men shared from their knapsacks. They could not risk a fire, so he must endure the cold and risk the possibility of death for the sake of the expedition. He was wrapped in blankets, and guards were posted. The officers deemed it necessary to wait for more ice to form. So the soldiers again waited in silence, very close to the enemy. They waited without fires all the next day and half the night again, until the moon was hidden. This time it was three in the morning by Charles's timepiece.

Captain Rogers, now recovered, and two of his Hampshire men set out for the lake to check out the ice. Within an hour they were back and the Captain pulled together the party. "The ice is still too thin to make it across and we can no longer risk detection by the enemy. We are going to head south and lay an ambush on the road from here to Carillon. Form up for march. I'll take two men with me as the lead. Captain Putnam, you take your Connecticut men as our rear. Mr. Smith, you have our right, and Ensign Johnson, you have the left flank. Quiet on the march, and keep your distances. Let's go."

Rogers veered more to the east than he had on their advance, so as not to take the same trail. Late in the afternoon they made it to just below a village that Rogers had set fire to on his last scout. Here they rested. About four in the morning the men were all prepared and they marched to about one and a half miles from the upper village near the fort. Rogers ordered the men to stash their packs in a barn on the point. The party then marched quietly through the barren fields to some vacant houses. Rogers ordered Captain Baldwin to keep twenty-three of the men with him in a house. Rogers, Putnam and Smith took the other men and hid in a barn about eighty rods northeast. They were hoping to ambush some farmers or herders coming to tend their animals or collect grain from the barns. With the men secure in their hiding places. Rogers and Smith went out to look for prisoners. They returned, not being able to find any enemy who were not within the cover of the guns of the fort. Both groups remained in their hiding spots the rest of the day until about nine that evening.

Captain Rogers called together the officer and NCOs that were with him and decided that no more time could be afforded and that they must make haste back to Fort William Henry. They decided to leave a message that they had been in the area, so Rogers ordered torches to be made. Every other man was to have a torch. "Keep together with a man without a torch to cover you. Ensign, you take five men with you and head for the houses. The rest of you, let's set fire to these barns." Then, on his order, they burst from the barn and in teams lay torches to the structures. Illuminated by the yellow and red flickering fires, men were scurrying through the grain-filled barns like locusts on fresh wheat. The torches and the burning of the barns were welcomed momentary warmth for their cold bones. Within minutes there was a bellowing from the burning barn they had been hiding in. It was human and McNeil and Cunningham rushed in with weapons ready to fire. Shortly, they emerged dragging, one of the rangers, an Indian who said he had fallen asleep. He was more black than brown from the smoke and soot of the fire. He was in great pain being burned on the legs severely. Rogers ordered several of the men to pick him up and carry him and they all made a dash toward the houses that were already being kindled by Johnson. When they arrived at the houses Rogers ordered them to continue on the run for quite a distance, as the blazing bonfires were sure to alert the enemy in the fort that there was foul play in their midst. Once in the forest again, they slowed their march and made it to some wetlands to rest. Turning around to see if the enemy was on their heels, they saw the sky had a red glow form the burning barns.

"Is everyone here?" inquired Rogers. "McNeil, see to making a litter for the Indian."

McNeil went to work fashioning a blanket between two poles.

Rogers knelt down and looked at the Indian's burnt legs. He shook his head. "We need to send off most of the men to find a quick route around Carillon. Captain Baldwin, I leave you to that duty. I'll keep Mr. Putnam, Smith and five others along with the Indian. We can move fast enough to get all home safely. Fill your canteens. Captain Baldwin, the men will starve if you don't get them back quickly. The first thing you must do when arriving at Fort William Henry is send down a bateau for us. Nurse, McNeil, Cunningham, Henry and Greenleaf, you seem to be better off than most, you're with me."

After a short rest, Captain Baldwin ordered the men back on their feet and they headed south, skirting the west shore of the lake. Soon after that, Rogers and the others set out as well.

They headed south and made it about eighteen miles, and then waded across Putnam Creek. The going for Rogers and his small party was slow and rigorous, having to take turns carrying the litter. Charles's stomach began to ache with the pain of hunger and it became difficult to keep up the strength to advance. At dark they could push forward no longer, and Rogers found them a clump of bushes to hide in to block the wind. They were close to the French fort. Captain Rogers and Putnam decided it would be prudent to take advantage of their closeness to the enemy fort, and they left the party and crept up toward Carillon. After a few hours they returned to the rest of the party.

Rogers was quietly chuckling. "Those Frenchmen will know I was here. I left them some signs that we have been here. We crept up and into the ditch of the fort. We were so close we could hear the voices of the guards. We must rest for a while and then we'll head out."

After about an hour they headed down to the water's edge and continued to follow the shore south. That night they made camp near where a large French party had camped the night before. While reconnoitering the area they found carved on a tree, "if they catch us they would burn us or we should them directly." The next two days were devastating to the men. They were under great stress to continue their march in the cold without fires, without food, and without energy, carrying the burned Indian through the snow. Finally, nearing the end of their strength, in the distance they saw a bateau approaching. Rogers stopped the march and the men lay and waited to see if it were enemy or friend. Then Rogers raised his musket and fired it into the air; it was the relief party. Quickly, the boat was rowed into shore and the men climb on board, they turned about and rowed back to the south.

The men were given bread and beef and some rum to wash it down. They devoured everything that was given them. One of the surgeon's mates from the fort was also with the boat and he attended the Indian and inspected the others' feet and hands for frostbite. The ride back was cold but they now had food. Their spirits were lifted and they now found time and energy for conversation.

"Nurse, you fared quite well out there," stated Rogers. "Have you done quite a bit of hunting back home?"

"Some, but not a lot. I have a small farm and work at one of the wharves. I did more hunting with my father and grandfather when I was younger," he replied.

"I am impressed. Are you interested in joining my ranger company when your enlistment is done? Or if I am able to persuade your commander to let you go would you be interested sooner?" asked Rogers. "We are going to be looking for men like you who can keep a good head on their shoulders and find their way around in the woods."

"I find your offer very flattering but I will have to think about it. Let me see how the spring goes and the campaign," said Charles with respect.

"I am going to recommend that you get a promotion anyway. You are worth more than a private's wage. I feel you should be leading men, not following them," offered Rogers.

"I would appreciate your kind words to Colonel Bagley or Captain Blake sir. Thank you," welcomed Charles.

The row in the bateau was much more comfortable and quicker than the winter forced march. It had possibly been the savior for some in the party. Shortly after midnight on the Sabbath they pulled into the bay and docked at the wharf at Fort William Henry. They had earned several days' rest.

OFF TO BOSTON

After a few good meals and some good nights' sleep, Charles and the other men of the scouting party resumed their regular garrison duties at Fort William Henry. About a week later, Charles was called in to the office in Colonel Bagley's house. Upon entering, he noticed several officers he had not expected to see there.

"Come forward, Mr. Nurse," ordered Bagley. Bagley, Captain Rogers and Captain Burk and Lieutenant Poor of Bagley's regiment all looked up. The officers were all seated at a table in the center of the room. "Nurse, I have just finished reading Captain Rogers' report. He stated that he has been impressed by your work on his scouting expeditions."

"Thank you, sir," replied Charles.

"For some time now, you have been working diligently on various duties within your own regiment. If you are asked to do woodworking, stand guard or even perform clerical duties you have shown yourself to be a man of honor and sincerity. Captain Rogers has asked that we consider transferring you into his charge as a ranger. At this time, I cannot and do not want to do this. You are too valuable of a man to lose from our Massachusetts companies. He has also asked, then, that I consider raising you in rank. In talking to Captain Burk and Lieutenant Poor, they are very pleased with your energy and experience within their company. At this time, Mr. Nurse, we are giving you a corporal's billet within my regiment. Your duties will be slightly different at present within our unit, though. I am dispatching you to serve temporarily with Captain Rogers. He can use your clerical expertise for a meeting that he has been ordered to attend. He has just received orders to march for Boston and meet with General Shirley. We are both of the opinion that your knowledge of the area and several key men of the town, would be of some assistance to the captain. Prepare your belongings. On your return I will expect a report from you and at that time I will make a decision as to your next duties. Do you have any questions, Corporal Nurse?" asked Bagley.

"Sir, I appreciate the kind words and thoughts of yourself and the other gentlemen. I will try my best to serve you sir, as corporal of your regiment. Thank you, sir," stated Charles enthusiastically.

"Very good, Nurse," said Rogers. "If you have no other questions, get your belongings together. We will be leaving via horse at sunset."

"You are dismissed, Corporal Nurse," ordered Colonel Bagley.

Charles snapped a salute, the officers returned it, and Charles turned about and left the office.

Within an hour Charles met Captain Rogers on the parade ground. Two horses had been readied for them and they tied their equipment and belongings onto the saddles, mounted up, and galloped down the road to the south. The two men made good time arriving in Boston on the fifth day. They went to the Bunch of Grapes tavern and rented a room for the evening, then enjoyed a warm meal and some refreshments. In the morning the two men rose early, dressed in their uniforms and went down to the keeping room and had a breakfast of bread, cheese and warm oatmeal. Then they headed out to meet with Governor Shirley. The day was mild for spring and it felt comfortable to be outside without wearing a greatcoat. The streets were already becoming congested as Bostonians headed for work and shopping. It was a great release from the rigors of camp and the fears of the war. Walking several blocks, Rogers and Charles came to Salisbury Street, and a short distance down the road they came to the State House. This was the hub of Boston. The State House was a stunning stone building of classic revival architecture. It was a three-story building with many large windows. A three-tiered cupola made it seem even taller. Charles and Rogers walked up to the steps and as Charles began to climb them, he looked up at the beautifully gilded horse and lion decorating the third story, just above the second story balcony. Being a time of war, there were two members of the Boston Independent Company of Cadets posted on each side of the large double doors. They were dressed very smartly in their scarlet coats with light buff facings and small clothes. When Rogers approached, the guards brought their muskets to present and Rogers returned their salute.

Entering the building, the men walked into a large room with very tall ceilings. The walls were lined with racks of muskets. On the right a clerk was seated at a large desk. The man addressed Charles and Captain Rogers. "May I help you, gentlemen?"

"Yes, Captain Rogers, of New Hampshire from Lake George. I have an appointment with General Shirley," answered Rogers.

The clerk responded as he stood. "Yes sir, I will tell the general that you are here." The man left the room and Charles and Rogers strolled about, looking at the marvelous room.

"This way, gentlemen," motioned the clerk when he returned. Looking at Charles, the clerk asked, "And you are who, sir?"

"Corporal Nurse, acting clerk to Captain Rogers."

The clerk then escorted Rogers and Charles up the stairs to a large office in the back of the second floor. They entered the room just as Shirley was dismissing another clerk.

"Your Excellency, may I present Captain Rogers and his clerk, Corporal Nurse," introduced the clerk.

Shirley rose from his chair and walked around his desk to shake Rogers' hand. "Greetings, gentlemen. Captain, it is a pleasure to meet you. Gentlemen, please take a seat."

"Sir, the honor is mine," replied Rogers.

"Gentlemen, may I pour you some of our good Boston rum?" asked Shirley graciously.

"Please," answered Rogers.

"Thank you, sir," replied Charles.

Shirley was a middle-aged Englishman who had come to the colony of Massachusetts-Bay over a decade earlier. He had made his reputation as a politician, statesman and general. His dress and appearance blended excellently to show off the epitome of his status.

"I am glad you brought the corporal with you. I have some orders for you that he should record." Charles took his writing tools from his haversack and began to take notes as Shirley began to talk.

"Captain, first off, I have drawn up this commission for you to recruit an independent corps of rangers." He handed a paper to Rogers. "You have done a good job, I see, from the dispatches your brother delivered several days ago. I believe that this new company will make your job easier. I intend that this company should consist of sixty men, all with great courage and fidelity, and accustomed to traveling and hunting. I am posting their pay to be three shillings York currency per day. Your pay would be raised to ten shillings a day, your lieutenants seven and your ensigns five. Each man will also be given ten Spanish dollars towards providing himself with clothes, arms and blankets. All are to be subject obviously to military discipline and the articles of war put forth by our great king. After recruitment, have the majority rendezvous in Albany and take whaleboats to Lake George. I envision your troops distressing the French and their allies by sacking, burning and destroying their houses, barns, barracks, canoes, and bateaux, and by killing their cattle. They should at all times endeavor to waylay, attack and destroy their convoys of provisions by land and by water."

The conversation continued for several hours, going very in depth into both their philosophies in the use of rangers. Rogers, being one of the most skilled and having a great deal of experience along the Lake George–Lake Champlain area, had very definite ideas. He was very opinionated as to his future plans for rangers as well. Both men left the meeting with great understanding of each other's intentions.

"I thank you for your time and understanding of my thoughts about our army's rangers, sir," said Rogers. "I feel that with your assistance that I can now go forth and do some real damage to our enemy."

"I have been hearing many good things about your work in the past four months. This is going to be a step in the right direction, in bringing the war to our enemy's doorsteps. I intend to draft letters to Colonel Whiting at Fort Edward and to Colonel Bagley at Lake George expressing my orders as to the use of your corps. Also, if you would this evening I would be pleased if you would accompany me to a meeting at our local Masonic lodge. It is meeting in the top floor of Faneuil Hall. If you agree, I will have my coach pick you up. Where are your accommodations?" asked Shirley.

"Sir, if I may, would it be alright if Mr. Nurse accompanied us as well? asked Rogers. He is of the lodge."

"Very good, it would be a pleasure to have another brother with us," stated Shirley.

"Then sir, we would be pleased to have the use of your coach," replied Rogers. Charles and Captain Rogers took their leave.

After dinner at the Bunch of Grapes the two men were picked up by Governor Shirley's coach and driven to Faneuil Hall on Salisbury Street. The coach stopped on the road outside the building. Charles had remembered its grandeur from his previous visits to the city. It stood two stories tall and was large compared to most buildings. It had many large windows and the bottom story windows were dressed with awnings. He glanced up and saw in the forming moonlight the brass grasshopper weathervane on top of the building. The two men entered the front doors and walked up the steps to the second door. At the door were two men with swords. Charles, being a Mason, knew the protocol and stepped forward. One of the men asked him a question and he responded appropriately, and he and Rogers were allowed to pass. Inside, several Masonic members of Boston greeted the men. Charles took an off-white pigskin apron from his haversack and tied it around his waist. As Rogers looked around the room he noticed all the men wore varying forms of these aprons as well.

Charles and Captain Rogers started talking to Luke Vardy, the tavern keeper of the Bunch of Grapes.

"Good evening, gentlemen. Mr. Nurse, I thought you might be a brother. Captain, have you not seen the light?" Vardy asked.

"I assume you mean, am I a member of the Masonic order? I must answer, unfortunately, no, sir, but I have often wondered how you become a Mason and would possibly consider it some day.

Another man walked over. "Captain, if I may, I would like to introduce myself. I am Benjamin Church, one of Boston's physicians. Your reputation precedes you, sir."

"I thank you sir, the honor is mine," replied Rogers.

"Brother Nurse, Captain Rogers," sounded Governor Shirley's voice from across the small room. "I am so glad you joined us. Make yourselves at home. There are some refreshments here on the table, enjoy yourselves. Captain, if you would accompany me I would like to introduce you to some others." Shirley escorted Rogers to a group of men.

"Brothers, I would like to introduce Captain Robert Rogers. I am sure most of you have read about him in the papers and gazettes."

"Gentlemen." Rogers stated in a charming voice as he bowed.

A lively conversation started as many of the men quizzed Rogers about some of his escapades with the enemy. While this was going on Shirley took several men aside and held a private conversation.

After several minutes Governor Shirley and the other men came back to the group.

"Captain, the Governor has given us some details as to your duties and the honorable job you have done for your king, country and God. You are to be commended, sir," stated Benjamin Hollowell, the Master of the lodge.

"Sir, you are most gracious to attend our meeting," added Ezekiel Price, the lodge's secretary.

"I am so impressed that such a gentlemen and courageous man who fights in God's name would bring firsthand information to us, you are most welcome sir," said Arthur Browne, the chaplain of the lodge and rector of Queen's Chapel.

"Gentlemen, thank you very much for your kind words and praise," replied Rogers.

"Captain," questioned Shirley, "we understand you were wondering about Masonry. We would like to offer you the chance, since you are away from the fighting momentarily, and it being some time before you may be able to return again to join our order. Would you consider coming into our lodge, sir?"

"Gentlemen, I am flattered. I consider it an honor," replied Rogers.

"It's settled, then," ordered Shirley. "Brother Nurse, would you and Mr. Pelham be so kind as to prepare the captain to be received?"

"Yes brother, it would be an honor," replied Charles.

"This way, Brother Nurse and Captain Rogers," guided Pelham.

"Brothers Otis, Ames, Perkins, let us all enter the lodge and prepare the ceremony for prospective Rogers," urged Hollowell.

The Masons entered their main ceremonial lodge room. It was ordained with the proper vestiges of Masonry and was beautifully furnished with lavish Jacobean furniture. The four men took their places at the points of the compass and within minutes Rogers was escorted into the room fully prepared. Questions were asked and answers given, signs and tokens were exchanged. Rogers was being given the honors rarely bestowed on others than sea captains disembarking on a voyage. Usually a Masonic member sponsored a new member and at a later date he could be brought into the lodge. A bag was passed and each man placed a token inside. A white cube meant acceptance, a black ball meant the prospective member would be denied. One black ball is all it would take. After collection the tokens were shown and Rogers was unanimously brought into the lodge that evening.

Early the next morning the decision was made that Richard, the Captain's brother, and Robert Rogers would move north and recruit for the new company. Charles was given furlough. He was ordered to meet Rogers in Starkstown New Hampshire, in three days.

Charles made a beeline for his home. Pushing his mount to its limit he galloped down the neck of Boston and up the post road leading north. The weather was good this day and Charles wasted no time. Onward he rode and late in the afternoon he turned the final curve before coming into Amesbury. He was ecstatic. He wanted so much to see his parents, brothers and Mary and her mother. From a distance he could see his father's farm, its rail and stone fences, the spreading oaks and the red clapboard of the house itself.

Charles slowed his pace to visually absorb what he could. Reining the horse into his parent's path he felt very safe and relaxed. He jumped off the horse and tied him to the hitching post behind the house. He could hear the grinding wheel whirling from the tool shed. Father must be sharpening his tools for the wharf, he thought. Charles walked over to the tool shed and opened the door. His father stood up from leaning over the wheel and looked towards the doorway with astonishment. "Charles, what are you doing here?"

"I was sent on a mission to Boston with an officer and he gave me a furlough for a few days. It was an unexpected surprise!"

"What's that on your shoulder? You a corporal now?" asked Caleb looking at the yellow shoulder knot on his uniform.

"Yes, sir, I just received my promotion before leaving. Where is everyone?" asked Charles.

"Mother is in the house preparing supper and William is not home yet from the wharf. Enoch..." Caleb was cut short. Enoch slapped Charles on the back.

"Hey, who is this soldier?" asked Enoch sarcastically.

"Enoch, how's my favorite brother?"

"Doing good, Charles," he answered as he held out his hand to Charles.

"What brings you home so soon?" Enoch quizzed.

"They sent me to Boston on business and I was given furlough for a couple days.

"How've my animals been?" asked Charles.

"Fine, you have six new piglets and two lambs. I am expecting that those that we don't keep will be ready to slaughter or sell in about six months."

"That's fine, Enoch. I can't believe how tall you're getting."

Enoch stood as tall as he could and measured himself against Charles.

By this time the three were ready to go into the house for supper. Charles walked through the back door first. His mother was ladling some soup from an iron pot hanging on the trammel over the fire. She looked up when she didn't hear a voice and saw Charles standing in the doorway.

"Charles! Lord be praised. You are home! Are you wounded?" she asked, in a very worried voice.

"No Mother, just here on a quick furlough," Charles answered. He walked over and gave his mother a hug and kiss. "It's good to see you, Mother."

"All you men, wash up and sit down for supper," she ordered. The three men quickly washed and took their seats. Then they bowed their heads and Caleb said the prayer.

"Lord Jehovah, we would like to take this moment to thank You for Your graciousness in allowing our son Charles to visit us after such a short time being away from us. We thank You oh Lord for taking care of him in his absence from us. Lord, we continually pray that you will bring this war to an end without many deaths this next campaign season and that You help us be victorious over Your enemies and their heathen. We also are approaching the spring planting season and ask that You see that we have ample rain and a warm spring so that our seeds will sprout and give us Your bounty. We ask this in Your name, A-men."

The feast that Martha had laid upon the table was grand and they was enjoyed every morsel. The family also had wonderful conversation. After dinner Charles helped his mother ret the table and sat for a little while and sipped tea with her. Then he excused himself to go and visit Mary and her mother. He left the house and mounted his horse and rode out the lane to the road and trotted to the next farm, a short distance down the road. This was Charles's own home, which he was letting Mary and her mother Sarah live in. John,

Mary's father and a good friend of Charles, had died from his wounds in the Battle of Lake George. Charles had thought often about Mary, his house and farm and what the future would hold for them after the war. He quickly saw his house with a pale glow in the windows from the candlelight. Hitching his horse to the post he walked up to the door briskly and rapped. He pulled his tricorn off and adjusted his uniform coat. The door opened and Sarah greeted him.

"Good evening, oh, it's Charles!" she exclaimed. Sarah took him by the hand and pulled him inside. There sitting side by side in front of the fire on an old bench were Mary and William, Charles's brother. They were chuckling, obviously enjoying each other's company. Charles was taken back. William was surprised. Mary was in shock.

"Charles," William blurted out. "You're home!" And he stood and walked toward his brother. Charles took his hand and also pulled him in closer, patting him on the back. Charles didn't know what to say.

Mary had gained her composure and walked over to Charles. She put her arms around his neck and gave him a long embrace. "It's so good to see you, I have thought of you daily," whispered Mary.

"Let's sit at the table and have a good talk. I'll heat some water for some chocolate. Sit, Charles," offered Sarah. They sat down and spent the next several hours talking about the last few months. Charles told them about some of his exploits. William told Charles about what was new around town and Sarah and Mary filled Charles in on the church doings and how things were around his farm. William also was more inquisitive about the war and what was being done about recruiting for the spring. At about ten, Charles and William decided they had better call it a night and begged their leave. Mary walked them to the door. She gave Charles a hug good night and offered to ride to town with him the next day. Then William gave Mary a hug and the two brothers mounted their horse and rode home. It was a quiet ride and when they got home Charles went quickly to bed. He was tired but also did not know how to take the new fondness between his brother and Mary. William was sixteen now and maybe Mary had feelings for him—she was closer to his age, after all.

The next morning Charles slept in a little, and by the time he arose his father and William had already left for work and Enoch was out tending to the cattle. His mother fixed him some warm mush and they sat and talked for about an hour. Then Charles hooked up the wagon and horse and went over and picked up Mary. They rode slowly down the wagon road along the Powow River and then turned north and headed through town. Things had not changed, but it was good for Charles to see home again. Periodically they would see friends and stop and talk. About noon, Mary stated that they needed to stop by the wharf, so they turned the wagon around and headed back down to the river. At Bagley's Wharf they stopped and got out, and walked into the boat shop. There were lots of Charles's friends and fellow workers all around the shop, and he spent time talking to all of them. It was lunchtime and most of the men were taking breaks. Mary, meanwhile, had walked over to William and had handed him a basket. He reached over and gave her a kiss on the cheek. Charles was stunned. William and Mary talked for a while and then she came over to Charles. The men started going back to work so Mary and Charles left and rode home back along the road.

"Why are you so quiet, Charles? Is there something you are not telling me? Has something happened at the forts that you are depressed about?" asked Mary, in a very concerned voice.

Charles took a side road up the hill behind the town. "No, I am just relaxing," he told Mary. He was becoming more confused but did not know what or how to bring it up to her. He thought he must observe more before making rash judgments. They took their time just riding up the hill then back down, and along the river back to the house. Then Charles dropped Mary off. She invited him over again and he agreed before leaving for his parents' house.

Charles's mother prepared another good meal for the family supper that evening, and again Charles left for an engagement with Mary. Shortly after arriving at the house, he suggested that he and Mary take a walk. He was relieved that his brother was not there. They walked and talked. Then Charles asked how his family had been.

"They have been doing very well. And they have been very generous to my mother and me. I have been a little worried about William though," answered Mary.

Charles stiffened. What was she going to say about William?

"We have become very close the past two months. He comes over every day or two and visits Mother and me. He often talks about the army and how he intends on enlisting. He has grown into a man, but I hate to see such young men marching to the war. I still can not block out the sights I have seen at Lake George."

"He talks about the war and the army when he visits you?" reiterated Charles.

"Yes, often," she answered.

Charles stopped walking and asked, "Do you think that he does not come just to visit you? Do you not find that strange? He seems to be more interested in you than two childhood friends."

"No, I do not find it strange that he visits my mother and me. Are you insinuating something?" responded Mary.

"Do you take him food every day at the wharf? The others there seem to be unsurprised at your appearance there," sputtered Charles.

"Charles Nurse, you are jealous!" scoffed Mary. "We have become good friends, nothing else. He has been very nice to us, and yes, I periodically take him leftovers if we have them. It is one of the only ways we have of returning his kindness."

"I apologize, I guess I am reading into it more than is real," offered Charles.

Mary took his hand and said, "No need to worry. I have the same feelings for you that I had before." They continued their stroll as the moon rose in the sky, enjoying the rest of the evening.

The next morning Charles rose early and spent time with his father and William as they prepared for work. He told William he would meet him for some lunch. Then when they left he spent time with his mother and Enoch before he left for chores.

Near noon Charles asked his mother to fix some meat, cheese and bread for him to take to his father and William. He left and arrived at the boat shop just before their break. He spent time talking to some of his friends and neighbors. Then he and William went out and found a tree to sit under. They threw down a blanket and sat, ate and talked.

"So, William, I hear you are still filled with the idea of joining the provincials?" inquired Charles.

"I sure am," William answered with dignity. "I feel it is my duty to head out with the recruits this spring. You have been enlisted for your second year now, and it's my turn now."

"I don't think you could classify it as your turn. Yes, I am going on my second campaign now, but I think that one reason I am serving is so you don't have to. You should not be thinking of such a thing for another two years," lectured Charles.

"It is legal now for me to enlist and I can do so without Father's permission," rebutted William.

"That is correct, you can enlist, but you must think about your future and our parents. I feel much better knowing that you remain here taking care of things that Father might not be able to. I know my leaving was a burden on him at times. You are a man now and capable of taking on the responsibility of an elder brother and son," offered Charles.

"I have tried my best to help both at home and by working here at the shop, but it is time to change my future. I intend to make some extra money before this war is over. I hear that they are going to offer a sizable bounty for enlistments next month. That, plus the pay will be far more than I can earn here. Then when I return I can get my own farm and prepare to settle down," said William proudly.

"Slow down. What do you mean settle down? You are only sixteen. You can look at maybe two to ten years before you settle down. What happens if you enlist and we have another major battle like the one last summer, the one that John Benjamin died in? It is hard enough keeping oneself alive, let alone keeping your friend or brother alive as well. I'm damned lucky that I wasn't killed!" expounded Charles.

"What do you mean, keep your brother alive! I can take care of myself. I have been firing a fowler for four years now and I can feed and take care of myself just fine!"

"Calm down, I know you can take care of yourself, but I would feel like I had to keep watch over you. You know that father and mother would expect it as well." Charles hated to say the next thing but he took a deep breath and said it anyway. "I also need you to stay and take care of Mary."

William looked at him. He paused then spoke again. "I will think about it, but I can not promise you anything."

"I guess that is all I can ask for," said Charles.

The two brothers finished eating, William went back to finish his work and Charles went back to the farm to get ready to leave. Late in the afternoon everyone met at Caleb and Martha's house. Enoch walked out of the barn with Charles's horse saddled and led it to the hitching post. They were all gathered around the back door. Charles was saying his goodbyes to everyone. He patted Enoch on the shoulder, shock his hand, then he gave his mother a hug. "I will write soon, Mother."

He shook his father's hand and they patted each other on the back. "Keep yourself well, son. We are always praying for you," said Caleb.

Then, turning to William he said, "Brother, please remember what we talked about. You need to set your priorities and stick to them." They shook hands and Charles looked at Mary.

She had a tear running down her cheek as she gave him an embrace and said, "My dear Charles. I can't wait for you to come home. I so want you here all the time."

Charles then whispered in her ear, "Please take care of William. He should not join the regiment. I will return, but I must continue to do my duty to my colony and our king. God will protect us. Now I must go."

He mounted his horse and started down the lane. Then reining the horse around, Charles waved one last time to all and smiled as he kicked the horse in the flanks and they lurched forward out the lane and onto the road leading north to New Hampshire. It had been a bittersweet visit. It would be some time before Charles could fully understand his entire visit.

BY WATER OR BY LAND

Charles rode all night, arriving in Starkstown around noon. He was quite distracted by parts of his visit back home, but he was under orders now and was not going to let his personal feelings interfere with his duties. He hitched his horse to the post in front of the local tavern. This is where Rogers had told him that they would meet. He walked into the building and was very surprised at how many people were inside.

It was a dark room, and men were standing and sitting all around. Captain Rogers was standing in front of the bar, and off to his right, at a table in front of the fireplace, was seated his brother, Richard. There were several others seated by him, and beside the table stood a rough-looking man who appeared to be nearing thirty years of age. He was almost six feet tall and was dark complected. His hair was long and he wore it untied. He was not well shaven either, giving him the air of being unkempt, as well as giving him a wild appearance.

Charles stood in the back of the room and listened. The man standing by Richard Rogers was giving quite a speech. He was obviously recruiting for Rogers and his new ranger unit. His words were clever and many men in the tavern apparently were interested. After his speech, he asked all interested men to come forth and enlist with Richard Rogers, the company's first lieutenant.

Charles walked over to Captain Rogers and reported in to him. He brought Charles up to date with his endeavors in recruiting.

"Who is the man who was talking to the townsmen when I walked in?" questioned Charles.

"His name is John Stark. He is to be my second lieutenant. My brothers and I have known him since we were boys. He's a good man and very experienced. How were things at home?" inquired Rogers.

Charles didn't want to go into detail so he answered, "I had a good visit and appreciate your giving me the time to do so."

After their recruiting meeting, Captain Rogers and Lieutenant Rogers headed up toward Fort Number Four. On their way they did more recruiting. By the middle of March they rendezvoused at Fort Number Four. Richard had thirty-seven men with him and Captain Rogers had seventeen. Richard was sent with his men toward Albany, and to finish recruiting on his way. Then he was to advance to Lake

George. Captain Rogers received orders to proceed to Crown Point with part of his new company and reconnoiter the area of the French and then to proceed for Fort William Henry. Captain Rogers and his party left on the morning of March 28.

About a week out on the march John Stark became ill, really ill. He could barely walk. So Rogers halted the column and had a fire built.

"I don't think I can make it to Crown Point and if I can, I will hold you back so severely that it will endanger your mission," explained Stark.

"You are right. I will assign a guard of six to accompany you to Fort Edward. If you take your time and if the men are diligent, you should have no problem getting there about the same time as we do. Select who you want to lead your guard. I am also sending Corporal Nurse. He has been out with us several times and is very capable. He also is skilled enough to be one of us," reassured Rogers.

"I will take my nephew, Archibald. He knows his way from here to the area of Fort Edward," suggested Stark.

Captain Rogers left Stark and his guard and marched north by northwest toward Lake Champlain. Stark and his men posted guards and then relaxed around the fire the rest of the day and night. For almost a week the seven men lay in the woods, trying to get Stark ready to continue. Then they headed out slowly to the west. The first week, their march was slow, and they could only travel short distances. Gradually Lieutenant Stark improved and they made it to Fort Edward. Then they were sent north to Fort William Henry.

Charles was placed on the point, as he was very used to the area between the two forts. About one-third of the way to Fort William Henry, Charles caught sight of a movement about 300 yards before him. He motioned for the column to halt while he and the other man who was with him went forward to investigate. Moving very slowly, Charles and the other man worked their way to the west, avoiding the road. At about 150 yards they stopped and knelt down behind some heavy brush. Peering deep into the woods before them they waited. Then Charles saw a movement again. It came from off to his left. For a moment he thought it was a deer, but they did not risk moving until they were sure. Then a few seconds later there was another movement that he saw from the corner of his eye back to the right, then another in front of them. Charles and the other man slowly brought their muskets up in a ready position. They were Indians; they were all over the area before them and sneaking about from tree to tree. It was very eerie watching them as they maneuvered. Charles and his partner dared not move! After about a half hour Charles sent the other man back to Stark to inform him of the Indian presence.

After a few minutes Charles's eyes focused on a bit of color by a large tree trunk. He tried to strain his eyes, and then he saw the silhouettes of two Indians looking directly at him! He froze and stopped breathing. He was by himself with no back-up, and who knows how many heathens were out there? He might be entirely surrounded!

One of the Indians moved and the other darted to another tree. With this movement Charles took the chance to lie down on the forest floor and cover himself with brush. He was terrified! Then he began to hear movement in the woods around him. It sounded like deer but he knew it was the Indians. He only prayed that Stark would come up and rescue him or that the Indians would not discover his hiding place. He continued to stay still but his body began to shake uncontrollably. For sure they would see the movement he thought to himself. Then suddenly, the movement became faint and gradually there was no more noise. Slowly he lifted his head and saw several Indians moving away from him about fifty yards off. He continued to wait and the Indians continued their animal-like movement like before. About ten minutes later Stark and the Charles's partner came up quietly and ever so slowly.

"Nurse, you alright?" Whispered Stark.

Charles could barely make himself answer. "Yeah."

"We were watching them. Looked like they were trying to find you," said Stark.

"I think we are safe now," offered Charles.

"Go ahead then, when you are ready let's move on. We need to make it up to the fort before dark," ordered the lieutenant.

After a few minutes the two men started off again leading the ranger party back toward the road and on toward Fort William Henry. They were very cautious, but made it about an hour before sunset. Charles was welcomed back to the garrison by his fellow Bay Colony men and he prepared a report for Colonel Bagley. Then after a hot meal he needed to relax so he retired to the barracks where several men offered to share a bottle of rum with him. Several hours later after he had warmed himself enough from the rum and the fire, and after he had caught up on all the things that had been gong on at the fort, Charles started to write a letter to his parents.

My dear Mother and Father,

I have just returned to Lake George. Captain Rogers did very well recruiting for his new ranger company. In New Hampshire we met up with a man, John Stark, whom Rogers took as one of his lieutenants. Stark was taken ill and I was sent with him and a small party from the Fort at Number Four toward Lake George. He was taken by a high fever and was quite debilitated. Stark appeared to be quite well trained in woods trekking and explained much about the natives. He told us that on a hunting trip in 1752, the St. Francis Indians took him captive.

It took us about five weeks to arrive at Fort William Henry, but little events occurred along the way. Today, I had lunch with Lieutenant Samuel Greenleaf. He told me of the things that happened while I was gone. Several weeks ago a group of eight rangers and provincials were sent out on a scout. That morning early, about 4 a.m., the sentries heard three or four scattered shots. Then they heard a large volley of almost a company of muskets. Mr. Baldwin of our colony, thinking it was the scouting party being attacked, sent Lt. Poor and nine men in two bateaux to find out. They left at six that morning and returned around two that afternoon. Samuel said Lt. Poor did find the scouting party and it had been beset. Lt. Poor brought in the bodies of Carlton, Bennet and Corporal McNeil of the rangers, of whom I have spoken. Greenleaf described how hideously men are treated in war. The bodies that were found were stripped, shot and scalped and cut in the most awful manner. One of them, McNeil was cut across his breast and then the savages turned the skin under his chin and left his innards exposed to the wild beasts! The others must have been taken captive, for no sign of them has been found.

The enemy has begun to act very bold. Samuel told me that Sergeant Darling went out with seven men. They reported that they saw many of the enemy on the lake and could hear others in the distance. Several of the enemy spotted Darling's scout and pursued them all the way back to within only a half a musket shot from the fort. A narrow escape and a blatant show of audacity by the enemy.

Shortly after the beginning of May, the provincial contracts ran out. There was a large group that had become upset with staying any longer. Word came in that no colony men had yet reached Albany to relieve our army. Grumbling started and problems became worse until a large group of men slung their packs and threatened to march for home. The colonel stopped the commotions and promised that relief was soon to arrive. He also soothed some animosities with an extra rum ration for the rest of the week. Soon a detachment of 80 regulars arrived to support and reinforce Fort William Henry. The next week 100 more regulars arrived with 120 provincials. They brought word that Gen. Johnson had a close encounter a few days ago in Albany. It seems a soldier's musket went off accidentally and hit Sir

William. Luckily, the ball passed through the sleeve of his coat and jacket and only grazed the skin of his breast.

I have been asked by Captain Burk of our regiment to accompany Lt. Poor on a scout tomorrow. Evidently, he wants a man of my experience to help out on such a scout. Lt. Poor is taking a party of 80 towards South Bay. I must prepare my gear and pack for my departure. Please give my fondest thoughts to Mary and her mother and my brothers.

> *Your loving son,*
> *Charles*

It was almost the end of May when Charles climbed aboard the bateaux to help lead the soldiers under Lieutenant Poor's command. There were eight boats and eighty soldiers. The weather was becoming quite nice and a slight fog rested on the bay next to the fort. The bateaux were shoved off and the men began to row out into Lake George. Nearly half of the detachment had been up the lake and felt comfortable on the expedition. Charles was in the lead boat.

About ten miles up the lake, Charles motioned for the small flotilla to turn into the outlet of a small creek. The draft on the bateaux was quite deep for such a shallow creek so the party could only make it easily up stream for about an hour. It was now mid-afternoon and the decision was made to land and conceal the boats. After doing this, the party was formed to march along the mountains to South Bay.

"Nurse," directed Poor, "You take five men and lead us to the bay. Lieutenant Brook, you take five of your Connecticut men and cover the right." The rest of the men were positioned on the left flank, rear guard and the main body. They marched for nearly two hours and the sun began to set. The march was halted, guards set and the rest of the men ate a cold dinner and made bush shelters to sleep. It was a pleasant night and the moon shone bright.

Just before daybreak Lt. Poor ordered Charles to go around and wake everyone. The troops all ate some food from their haversacks and set out again up the creek. The terrain was becoming very swampy so the men began to slow their speed. Charles was again on point with his hand-picked squad.

Suddenly there was a flash of movement off to the front right of Charles's forward position. He quickly stopped the advance and sent a man to send Lieutenant Brooks and his men from the right flank. Everyone found cover and waited to see what the movement was. From his vantage, Charles could see the movements of the Connecticut men as they inched forward. Lieutenant Poor came up from the main body of men and joined Charles. "What have you seen?" asked Poor.

"There was some movement off to the right, sir," responded Charles. "I could not make out what it was, so I sent word for Lieutenant Brooks to reconnoiter."

"There," pointed Poor. "Just before the Connecticut men."

Charles and the lieutenant ducked down even lower and peered into the distance. A subtle movement caught their eye. They could just make out the face of an Indian peeking out from around a fallen tree stump. As they watched Lieutenant Brooks and his men twisted their way closer to the enemy's position. Unfortunately, Brooks' party had not seen their foe. The other soldiers in Lieutenant Poor's party were at this time virtually helpless. Suddenly, the woods erupted with musket fire before Brooks and his men rushed forward with great speed. They ran directly into the middle of the enemy ambush. Surprisingly, the Indians took to flight and Brooks and his men gave chase. At this moment Lieutenant Poor motioned for the other men to move up toward the enemy as well. Then suddenly there was another eruption of musketry about a hundred yards farther in the direction that Brooks had charged. There was a great commotion from the woods and a continued musket fire that gave the main body of provincials the idea that a massive group of the enemy had struck Brooks.

"Push forward, men!" yelled Poor, and Charles and the others sprinted toward the gunfire.

The broken terrain hampered their efforts to reach the area of the gunfire. Then again, Charles saw the Indians and the Connecticut men. The Connecticut men were retreating and this time the Indians were skirting around the far left flank of the provincials.

"Where is your lieutenant?" Shouted Poor.

One of the breathlessly reported, "He was in the lead, charging the heathen. We were surrounded and with all the smoke I could see only his back as he leaped onto one of the Indians. Then three natives jumped on him and we took to our heels."

"Nurse, take your men forward. Careful, they might still have an ambush for you," ordered Lieutenant Poor.

Charles and his men moved farther into the woods. They advanced step by step. There was no movement ahead of them. Then Charles and the others spotted the lieutenant. It was grotesque! Charles ordered his men to form a perimeter to watch for the enemy, sent one man back for Lieutenant Poor and Charles knelt down by the body. It was one of the most revolting things he had ever seen. The Indians had made a quick mutilation of Brooks. They had not only scalped him but also had cut his mouth open, cut his tongue out, and slit his belly open! Then they had crammed his entrails into his mouth! Charles unrolled the lieutenant's blanket and draped it over the body. Lieutenant Poor came up and lifted the blanket and almost gagged.

By this time, with the barbarity of the savages, the lieutenant decided that the best course was to fall back to the fort. "They must be after our boats. There are too many of them so our only choice is to make haste over land back to Fort William Henry."

Leaving the body, the provincials headed back to the west, making sure to avoid the lake's shore. Lieutenant Poor set guards but they were moving at such a pace that if they were attacked it would make no difference. Most of them at this point were terrified.

About the time they were almost back to the fort, musket fire started. It was not far from the fort so Lieutenant Poor led his men south of the area. The firing stopped quickly and the lieutenant ordered Charles and the others to march directly to the fort. When they arrived, Lieutenant Poor reported to Colonel Bagley. Meanwhile, there was talk amongst the soldiers. Charles learned that some Indians had attacked a wood cutting party a short distance from the fort and that was the firing they had heard.

Bagley ordered Captain Rogers out after the Indians with 170 men. Charles and most of the returning soldiers had had enough soldiering for the day and chose not to go with Rogers.

Charles and most of the party were quite shaken from what they witnessed. For the next several days Charles was charged with working on some of the boats being completed for expeditions north. He spent most of his time working on a liter. This was a heavy masted craft being built to transport stores and artillery up the lake.

On June 6, Rogers pulled together his provincial company from the winter garrison. He addressed his men. "Gentlemen, you have done a great duty to your colonies. You have followed me with great loyalty, and for that I am very grateful. The end of your enlistments has come. Our orders were to harass the enemy this past winter and early spring. We have done so very well. General Shirley has given me new orders. As you know, he has charged me with recruiting a new company of rangers for this year's campaign. Lieutenant Rogers and myself have been very successful in this endeavor. At this time you have the right to leave for home, but if any of you wish to stay on with us I would be honored to enlist you in our newly formed company. I apologize for you receiving no pay. I have attempted to secure money's for your but to no avail. Knowing how disgruntled many of you are I do not find it incorrect for you to leave. For those of you who may choose to stay on I will promise you that I have already been promised funds from General Shirley and that I will do everything in my powers to continue to grievance the need to pay you for your winter's service."

The rangers talked amongst themselves. Many were angered by the audacity of the colonies. They had done service expecting compensation. Finally, the majority of the winter company slung their packs and marched off for home. Only fourteen chose to remain and join the newly formed company. Rogers now had sixty-seven officers and men under his command.

Scouts continued going out daily. Rogers led a party of thirty-six on the thirteenth and Lieutenant Greenleaf took another party on the fourteenth. Scouts were going everywhere. The preliminary work for a large campaign was being done, but still there were no large formations of troops arriving at the lake.

Charles and Gideon Lowell were diligently inletting mortises for the some of the liter's planking when they heard a great commotion at the fort's gate. They had been listening to the rhythmic beating of a drum in the fort as several prisoners were receiving punishment lashes. The two prisoners had been found guilty of desertion. Charles and Gideon stopped their work, as did the other men on the wharf. They watched as a large group of about 100 men marched out the gate and down the path. As the party made it down the hill from the fort and turned to head down the military road it became clear what the commotion was. In the center of the crowd were the two soldiers who had been stripped of their uniforms and wore only their breeches and shoes. Their hands were bound and they were being led down the path like animals. About their necks were horse collars, an attempt of the army to shame the deserters and make sure no others in the ranks would attempt desertion. As they turned and walked toward the woods Charles saw the blood of their whippings streaming down their backs.

The next day was the Sabbath. After breakfast Thomas, Gideon, Charles and Joseph Nichols went over to view the ground where the fight was last year. They stood on the area where the far right of Johnson's army defended themselves. This was the ground that their regiment had fought on and stopped the flanking attempt by the French and Indians. As they scanned the ground it was almost as if nothing had ever happened. The visual scars of the battle had been erased and even more of the woods had been cut back towards the south. Behind them now stood a great fort, and the entrenched camp had expanded and now had a permanent wall around it for firing.

After a short while the men strolled over to the burial grounds from the great battle. They knew exactly where to go to find the Massachusetts burials and stood in reverence. The grave of Colonel Titcomb had a fine wooden plank for his grave marker, but the soldiers only had simple wooden shingles. It was a solemn moment for these men who had lived through such a troubling experience.

From down the road came the sounds of cattle and the creaking of wooden wheels. Whips cracked and the voices of wagoners urged their teams forward. First, into the clearing came a party of provincial rangers. They obviously had been the forward guards for the supplies. Then within moments a long caravan of wagons being pulled by oxen lumbered into view. There were sixty-five wagons in all, loaded with stores for the upcoming trek north. This was becoming a daily occurrence. Some days there were hundreds of wagons arriving and returning back for more loads of supplies, boats, ammunitions and food. It would just be a matter of time now and an army would be formed on this very spot. Time was waning fast though. Men were needed, training would be necessary, and still there was no sign of reinforcements. Would they arrive in time?

OVER THE MOUNTAINS

Early the next morning at formation, Charles was instructed to report to Captain Burk. The captain ordered him to make ready for a scout under the command of Captain Rogers. He was to take with him Thomas and Joseph. They were to draw provisions for six weeks! This was to be the longest scout to date. Charles wondered if they were going all the way to Quebec City.

Rain fell steadily all day and made it difficult to pack the boats and still keep provisions dry. Just before dusk Sergeants McCurdy, Moore and Burbank began calling the soldiers together for their departure. They were formed up on the beach near the wharf, fifty men in all. The sergeants quickly counted the men off into five squads and hustled them into the five awaiting whaleboats. Roger was still on shore giving final orders to John Stark, who was being left in charge of the remaining rangers. Rogers turned about and bounded into the first boat, motioned to the others and they pushed off in unison, rowing out into the bay of Lake George. The sunset was brief because of the overcast skies, but the rain now had stopped.

As they continued to row, Charles found that he was in the boat commanded by Sergeant Jonathan Burbank. He was new to Rogers' Company but Charles was to learn that he had much experience. Beside Burbank, Thomas and Joseph, the boat also held Thomas Cunningham and James McNeil, who now was a private instead of corporal.

"Nurse, you're the corporal in this damned boat, so you'd better be make'n sure that everyone toes the line," ordered Sergeant Burbank. McNeil and Charles looked at each other but both of them knew better than to say a word.

The men rowed with great enthusiasm, trying to make at least ten miles before it became too late that night. After about four hours, they had made it to the first group of islands and Rogers had the soldiers conceal their boats and rest for several hours.

The next morning Rogers and his men set out on Lake George once more. They had only traveled about five miles and Rogers ordered them to land on the east shore. The men were told to bring the whaleboats onto shore and after doing so Rogers called them all together.

"On my last scout I discovered a way to deceive the enemy and put us to an advantage. It will take great fortitude but I feel that if we accomplish this mission we will have the upper hand. What I intend to do is move these boats to South Bay. From there we can have full access to Lake Champlain and the northern forts of the French." Many of the men looked at each other in wonderment. "What we will do is carry them over that mountain." He pointed at the mountain behind them.

"Captain, sir," interrupted Thomas Cunningham, "We have followed you from one end of Lake George to the other and from one fight to the next, but how in the hell do you expect us to get these boats over a mountain?"

Rogers picked up a stick and rested it over his shoulder. "I intend for us to pick them up and carry'em and carry'em, drag'em or what ever else it takes. We have plenty of muscle, rope and ample brains. We have men who are used to hard labor and skilled at block and tackle. It should just be another job to us." The men looked up in mild disbelief. No one said anything about not being able to do it, though.

"Ensign, you and the sergeants take control of this and have some men climb up about four rods and tie off some ropes. Then get into those tarps in boat number one. I had some blocks placed in the boat. Rig up a block and tackle system and get'em to hauling. I'll take Richard and McNeil with me. We're going to the top to make sure nothing has changed. Make sure to place guards so you aren't snuck up on. We'll be back about dusk," directed Rogers.

Rogers, his brother and McNeil scurried up the side of the mountain and in no time were hidden within the forest. Ensign Johnson began to give his orders. "Henry, you take five men and watch for the French. Sergeant McCurdy, take five men and get some ropes tied off to sturdy trees. Sergeant Moore, take ten men and get the blocks out and figure out how we're going to rig this up. Sergeant Burbank, you take fifteen men and unload those boats. Make sure to conceal everything well. We'll come back for our stores once we're on the top. The rest of you men, take everyone's gear and stow it away up there by where we are pulling. We'll have to drag it along with us as we advance from spot to spot."

The rangers made short time out of getting everything ready to go. Then Ensign Johnson prepared them to start their advance up the mountain. "Alright, We'll move one at a time. Ten of you on each side of boat number one. The rest of you on the two ropes rigged to pull her. Ready, then, pull! Heave! That's it, men, push that boat! Keep it up men! Watch those rocks! We want a bottom in her when we get to the water on the other side!"

The men shoved and pulled with all their might. Finally, about dusk, the captain came back as they were just finishing up with the last boat.

"Good, you seem to have things all arranged. Four rods today, if we can do fifteen tomorrow and the next day we will be able to slide the boats down the other side and launch'em by Saturday. You will need some rest now, though. McCurdy, set up a guard for tonight. Half of the men awake at all times. No fires. It's looking cloudy, so it shouldn't get too cold tonight. Have the men eat and rest. I want to be up before daybreak," delegated Rogers.

Just before dawn Rogers awoke his men and got them off to an early start. This was strenuous work. The weather was warm and the insects were surrounding them like an entire tribe of Abenaki, but there really was no way to fight this enemy. Several times during the day it rained but then cleared, just to bring more humidity to their already torturous working conditions. Then, just as the sun was setting, they reached the summit with all of the boats.

The next morning, parties of men were sent down to bring up all the detachment's supplies. Then rigging the block and tackle to lower the boats, they began the long slide down to the bottom of the mountain. This was a different effort, trying to keep the boats from careening down the mountain and bashing to a million pieces. The rangers used every trick in the book and all the leverage and muscle they could. Their hands were raw; they were sweaty, dirty and exhausted. But, by late in the afternoon they had the boats and the supplies down to safety.

The soldiers took a short rest as Rogers and two others scouted the area and looked for the optimum area to launch their vessels. It was only about an hour and Rogers and his party came back.

"We're almost there now." Rogers pointed to the northeast as he continued. "Just over that little knoll is a small bay which flows into a little tributary of South Bay. From there we can take the war all the way to Quebec if we wish. We must be extra cautious from here on, this is the same area that the French send many of their raiding parties through, south to Fort Edward. Leave a guard on the supplies and let's get as many men as possible under each boat and carry them over to the water."

One by one the men flipped the whaleboats upside down and strained and lifted them onto their shoulders and marched them over to the little bay. The area of the bay was not much larger than a half mile in circumference. It was a low spot nestled into the mountains that was lush and green with many cedars growing around its perimeter. The mountains rose sharply to the west from where they had just come and to the east was a very slight rise of ground covered in poplars. If it were not for the necessity of caution it would have been a beautiful place to relax.

With everything loaded, the men took a short rest and then set off toward South Bay. The tributary was very narrow at this spot and the boats could only travel in single file. They were very close to shore, making every man in the company extremely nervous of an ambush. Then the rivulet opened out and eventually they rowed into South Bay. Here Rogers ordered the men to keep single file and enough distance only to be able to see the boat before them. They skirted the western shore until they came to a narrows and they entered a river. At this spot Rogers had the flotilla move to the eastern bank and continue north. They now were on Wood Creek. The rangers continued rowing all night, keeping a watchful eye for any advanced parties of the enemy. With all the strenuous labor of the past three days, rowing all night made the dark hours seem forever.

Just before the sun began to show itself, Rogers ordered all the boats to put to shore. There was a tiny creek leading off on the west bank. The rangers rowed their boats into its mouth and pulled them on shore and concealed them.

"We are only about six miles from Carillon now. We cannot risk continuing any farther in daylight. McCurdy, post a guard. I want a picket line and a roaming guard as well. Half of you get some sleep, the other half on guard at all times." Safely concealed, the men spent the entire day without seeing any enemy.

That evening, the men were all roused and the whaleboats again were launched. After an hour they came close to Carillon. Rogers quietly issued orders to travel single file but keep the boats very close together. They were to be extremely quiet. Slipping by the fort, Rogers and his party could easily make out the fires and at one time just off the point of Ticonderoga Rogers even made out the enemy watchword as guards were being switched. By the number of fires around the fort he judged there must have been an army of at least 2000 men encamped. Under the cloak of darkness, Rogers and his party continued through the thin 400-yard narrows and inched their way farther north into Lake Champlain. They had gone about five miles and the flotilla was ordered to the eastern shore and to conceal the boats. Daybreak was almost upon them again and they were in the middle of enemy territory. Travel during the day would be suicide. In the morning it rained. In the afternoon the rangers observed only a few bateaux coming down the lake. Unexpectedly, there was little movement on the lake.

That night Roger's men embarked once more. Their mission was to pass Crown Point, but the night was very starry and the moon shone so bright that Rogers thought it prudent to lay on shore through the evening. Therefore, the rangers reached a point of land, dragged their boats ashore, concealed themselves, and rested.

The next day there was much more traffic and about a hundred boats were traveling south. The rangers lay motionless, just observing. Suddenly, seven boats came into sight and began to veer toward the eastern shore. They were aiming directly for Rogers and his hidden party. Had they been seen? The rangers checked their weapons and made ready to receive the enemy. They became motionless. The enemy came so near Charles could hear their voices. One man, a French officer, seemed to be directing the small flotilla, and the boats passed the point of land where the rangers hid. They were not out of danger yet for the French landed their seven boats only 150 yards from Rogers' party.

Rogers, Charles and the others dared not move. The enemy disembarked and several of the officers from the boats found a shaded spot on the shore and their soldiers unloaded a trunk and laid out a small feast. Wine, bread, cheese and some sort of meat were being served. The French were quite jovial here in the area that they thought was so safe. After about an hour they packed up as quickly as they had landed and shoved off toward Carillon.

That night about nine they once again took to the water. This night it was overcast enough and Rogers and his men rowed north and slipped past the French post at Crown Point. Rogers' party felt much safer being past the fort. They made good time and continued on about ten more miles that night before going ashore and concealing the whaleboats for the coming daylight.

Again, the soldiers in Rogers' party lay in hiding all day. There was also considerable traffic on the lake. This time the rangers saw some of the French might, when a group of thirty boats passed their hiding spot. This time a schooner accompanied them! This group of watercraft was heading toward Canada.

At evening, Rogers ordered his men to row on down the lake. They were able to make about fifteen miles and Rogers had them land. "McCurdy, you take Cunningham, Henry and Holt and reconnoiter by land. See what you can find north of us. Mr. Johnson, have the rest of the men formed into a guard and have half of them resting," instructed Rogers.

Shortly after daybreak, McCurdy came back into camp and reported to the Captain. "Sir, that schooner that passed us is only about a mile from us. We can take her, she is at anchor!"

"Ensign, lighten those boats and let's get in the water! We have a prize to catch!" exalted Rogers. The soldiers scurried about, making sure nothing other than weapons would belabor their venture.

"Sir, on the water," exclaimed McNeil, who was standing guard on the water's edge. Rogers reeled about and saw two lighters, or small shallops, heading directly for them.

"Everyone, prepare to fire on them!" yelled the captain. The men immediately formed from the cover of the shore and took careful aim. The lighters intended to land at their position. Rogers barked the order, "FIRE!" The fusillade was well place and several of the enemy dropped. Then in French, Rogers hailed the French officers, offering them quarter if they came ashore and surrendered. For a moment, it appeared that this was to be a simple task as a voice from one of the lighters answered that they would obey. Then the two lighter turned about and sailed for the opposite shore.

"To your boats, I'll not have them get away that easy!" yelled Rogers. The rangers sprang into the whaleboats and shoved off chasing the lighters. Overtaking the lighters, half the rangers from each whaleboat boarded the lighters and forced a quick surrender. After taking a quick count there were twelve of the enemy, three who had been killed in Rogers' opening volleys, two wounded, one severely.

"See what is in those kegs and bags, McCurdy!" insisted Rogers. "Sergeant Moore, have those prisoners bound and separated until I can talk to them. Give me this one," ordered Rogers. He took him by the neck and began to pummel the Frenchman's face. "You tell me were you came from and where you are headed or I'll have you shot on the spot!" screamed Rogers. "Monsieur attendre, I am corporal of Marines. There are 500 more Marines coming in this direction. We are leading the way," reported the Frenchman in very broken English.

"Sergeant Burbank, see to the wounded. They have to be able to travel now!" The rangers were all over the two ships like ants on molasses. With everything secure Burbank reported that one of the prisoners was mortally wounded. "We can't have a wounded man left behind to tell all of France what we are doing, knock him in the head, then he won't bother us," directed Rogers. Then pulling the large knife from behind his back Rogers knelt down and scalped the three dead men. "Make sure to get his scalp, too, Burbank. Get the rest of them in our boats. We are going to have 500 angry Frenchmen here very quickly if we do not get out of here! Take some of those kegs of wine and brandy and put them in my boat. Sergeant McCurdy, get these scows ready to sink. I cannot leave such a feast of good spirits, wheat and flour for the enemy. Everyone else, in the boats!" ordered Rogers.

The men quickly followed Rogers' orders, McCurdy jumped into his boat, and the rangers rowed toward the south. When they shoved off the two ships began to sink slowly, McCurdy and several men had hacked large holes in their keels. The men dug their oars deep into the water and pulled their whaleboats with long steady strokes toward the south. Several miles away, Rogers ordered them to the east shore. "McCurdy, Moore, get the boats unloaded except for those two kegs. Have the men fill them with stones and sink them. All of you remember this spot. We'll be back for them and those spirits will be very refreshing on future marches," ordered Rogers.

The men quickly followed the orders and began a hasty march back to Fort William Henry. For three days, the party traveled with great speed. They were becoming very exhausted and their food had dwindled to the wheat and flour they had taken from the French vessels. Evaluating his party, Rogers issued the following orders. "Lieutenant, many of these men will not make it back to the fort at this pace. They cannot march the rest of the way either. We need boats. Take Sergeant McCurdy and a dozen volunteers and march directly to William Henry. Report to the colonel and get back to us with great urgency with a party of thirty men and ten boats. I will keep the rest of them alive but you must hurry."

Charles and eleven others volunteered to march with the lieutenant and they left almost immediately. These men were also very tired but pushed themselves and marched to Fort William Henry within three days. Lieutenant Rogers went directly to the office of Colonel Bagley and requisitioned the boats needed. He then rallied together the rangers that had been left at the fort and quickly headed down the lake to rescue his comrades. Charles and the others were ordered to stay and, once recovered, to return to their units and that Rogers' men were to form scouting parties as needed by Colonel Bagley. This had been an exhausting expedition but Charles thought how grand a coup it was to be able to place British boats on Lake Champlain. Charles relaxed and took time to write his parents a letter.

My dear Mother and Father,

Some headway has been made in advancing toward the enemy forts here at Lake George. I just returned from an exhausting march to the far north. There were a large number of us under the command of Captain Rogers. We traveled in specially made whaleboats for Rogers' usage. They were very serviceable. We had advanced to Lake Champlain and were observing enemy boats on the lake, two lighters came into view, and we fired on them, captured the two boats, killed four, and took eight prisoners. The captain separated the enemy prisoners and at our camp on the 7th called for me to scribe some interrogations. We found out some very pertinent information. The Frenchmen stated that a great deal of regular enemy soldiers and militia were rendezvousing at Fort

Chamblee and were expected daily to advance to Carillon. They were beginning to stockpile a great deal of stores, some of which we captured in the lighters and sunk. The prisoners also stated that a new general was leading the troops destined to drive against our forts. In addition, he had arrived recently from France with two regiments. They also told us that a party of 300 French and some Indians were already in position to distress our forts and attack our convoys of these stores all up the Hudson River. Reports were that the enemy government was offering rewards of 60 livres for English scalps and 50 crowns for English prisoners. One of the Frenchmen also stated that they were expecting a good harvest in Lower Canada for this fall, but they had been hurt slightly by an epidemic of the pox. To our amazement, one of the prisoner's names was Greenleaf! I do not think that he and Samuel are relatives but when Samuel called him cousin the man felt much safer.

Many other parties have been venturing out to reconnoiter the enemy and scout for the best routes to attack. We have also launched a lighter here at Fort William Henry. Men have started to come in, but not in great enough numbers to make for a sizable attack. The enemy is expected to have nearly 3000 men now stationed at Carillon.

Today dispatches came up from Fort Edward. It seems that General Winslow of our colony and General Lyman of Connecticut have arrived with a large number of troops and artillery. General Winslow has given orders to Colonel Bagley to make ready all sloops, lighters and bateaux. We now have two ships between twenty and forty tons and have two of almost forty tons that will be ready to launch within ten days. We are waiting for rigging to get here from New York.

I have rested for several days now and I must return to duty. I have been ordered to help finish one of the large sloops. Captain Rogers has been ordered to raise another company of rangers. His brother, who I have spoken of, is to command it. It was filled very quickly, but I have decided to remain in the ranks of the Bay Colony.

Please give my best to Enoch, William, Mary and her mother.

Your Loving Son,
Charles

REINFORCEMENT

AND REUNION

On Thursday Charles was ordered to prepare his squad of Massachusetts men for an honor review for a general arriving from Fort Edward. He made sure his men were dressed in freshly brushed uniforms and that all their gear and accouterments were clean and in good working order. Shortly after noon a runner came into camp advising the officers that a large detachment was on the road about a mile outside of camp. The drums began to beat assembly and men began to rush from all areas of camp. The regiments were formed on the ground between the swamp and the fort. Sergeants and corporals barked commands and the officers began to congregate before their respective units. All quieted within the ranks and off at the edge of the woods Charles could hear the rhythmic beating of drums. Colonel Bagley and his field officers marched out the front gate of Fort William Henry and took their positions before the entire assemblage. "Finally," Charles thought, "a sizable troop of reinforcements has arrived. Now we can move toward the enemy forts."

A group of about fifty rangers jogged into the clearing and fanned out, covering the opening. Then, emerging in the lead of the column, came a middle-aged officer riding a shiny black horse. He must have been a man of importance, for his scarlet uniform was adorned on every seam with sparkling gold braid. In the procession just behind him was a group of six other mounted officers, and just behind them marched several military regiments. There were men from several colonies. One could tell from where they hailed: from the blue-clad boys of Massachusetts to the red-uniformed lads of Connecticut. As soon as each regiment entered the clearing the flag ensigns unfurled their colors.

Charles's unit was directly behind Bagley and his field officers, so when the general and his entourage dismounted he could faintly hear the officers' conversation.

"General Winslow," stated Bagley, "I am glad to see that you and your reinforcements have arrived. I have made all the preparations you requested. I know you will want to refresh yourself before reviewing the troops. But if I may, Sir, in your honor I have ordered a firing of the fort's artillery."

"I am glad we have finally arrived. I will only need a few moments to direct my sergeant major for ye instruction of the placement of my belongings on the lead wagon following us. So, sir please feel free to fire your salute," replied Winslow.

Bagley turned to an officer standing by the fort gate and commanded, "Fire the salute!"

From inside the fort the commands were heard, "Prepare to fire, FIRE!" With thunderous roars nineteen cannon were fired in sequence. Fire and pillars of soft white smoke belched from each muzzle as the charges erupted from each cannon.

General Winslow saluted Colonel Bagley and Bagley and his field officers returned with proper military etiquette.

"Sir, if I may, this way to your quarters," Bagley directed with a wave of his right arm. The field officers, Bagley, Winslow and his officers all marched from the field and entered the fort parade ground.

After the field officers were out of sight the Brigade Major stepped forward and instructed a sergeant major to direct the reinforcements to the positions where they were to set up their camps, and he then dismissed the garrison to their duties. Charles was ordered to report for clerical duty at the colonel's office. He quickly went to his barracks and fetched his quill, inkpot and orderly book and reported to his duty. At each side of the door to the colonel's office stood a guard with fixed bayonet. He entered the room and walked to the rear, and sat at the long table for the clerks. Opening his book and wetting his quill, Charles was prepared just in time for the officers to begin speaking.

Colonel Bagley was first to speak. "Sir, if I may? Our garrison has been hard at work since last fall finishing the fortifications set forth here by Mr. Eyre, His Majesty's engineer. We have been actively building bateaux as well, and also have several ships for your service. At present I have four ships, two just over twenty tons and two of forty tons ready to launch. We are at your disposal, Sir."

"Colonel, I commend you and ye work of your garrison. Though you have made good progress here at Lake George, the army has not formed quick enough to reinforce your garrisons here and at Fort Edward for an early advance on the enemy. Generals Webb and Abercrombie are at Fort Edward with part of the regulars. Lord Loudoun is now at Albany with the rest of the regiments. I have brought 2,000 of our provincials to finish preparations for our advance. To be honest with you, gentlemen, there have been some discussions that I must pass on to you. It is in regards to the fielding of the king's regulars and our own provincial troops. Knowing the extent of the feelings of the vast majority of the field officers of our colonies, I attempted reasoning with General Abercrombie on the settling of ranks. I told the general; personally I would be pleased to follow whatever orders were to be given. I also mentioned that it was very possible that the soldiers of the colonies would desert in droves if placed under regular, rather than colonial command. Our men are enlisted expressly for this campaign under our command and if any deviation is made upon them and their contracts, it is the opinion of the provincial officers that the greater part of the army would be disillusioned and that the majority of the colonies would in the future have grave difficulty raising sufficient troops to support other expeditions. Furthermore, it was brought up that this army is an organized body and that as such it would be an interference to place our officers under that command of regulars. The general expressed Lord Loudoun's ideas that our provincial officers were to rank beneath those of his field command, placing even myself below his colonels and majors. This settling of rank is not a battle we wish to take up for this campaign season; the movement toward the enemy fortresses is battle enough for one campaign!" preached General Winslow.

For several hours there was a lively discussion on possible problems with regulars and provincials serving together. The field command officers also had many question for the preparations for their units' movements north. There was also much time spent conferring over the security of the supply trains and troop marches between Albany and Fort Edward and on to Fort William Henry. Finally, a little before three o'clock, Charles and the other scribes were dismissed.

After returning to his barracks Charles began to prepare the rations for his mess. Just as the food was finished, Thomas, Gideon, and Joseph showed up. They ate and then decided to take a walk over to the entrenched camp and see if any of the Massachusetts men who marched in with Winslow were anyone they knew. The four men left the fort and walked over to the camp. The soldiers had erected their tents in good order and a sea of white canvas stretched within the log redoubts of the entrenched camp. As Charles and his mess mates strolled down the streets between the tent rows, most of the soldiers were relaxing after a day's march. When they arrived at the Massachusetts camps, they each started seeing a few men they knew from back in Amesbury and other nearby towns. Suddenly, Charles was knocked in the back, hard. He stumbled forward and wheeled around with his fists clenched! With adrenalin instantly pumping through his body and his eyes piercing forward to the man who hit him he became stunned, stunned with surprise. There stood a handful of young men, barely of age, grinning, chucking and nudging each other like young boys do. In the center of them was a familiar face; it was William, his brother!

"What in God's name are you doing here!" yelled Charles.

"Come to join you and the other men, to kill Frenchmen!" replied William with his chest puffed out and a smirk on his face. He looked like a prized rooster strutting in the hen house.

Charles was dumbfounded. "Do mother and father know? Did they allow it? Why would you come here?"

"Well brother, I told you that I would be joining you in this war. When the recruitment officers showed up to fill the levy I thought hard about staying, but there was an urge down inside that I had a duty to march out with the others to keep the French from our frontier. I figured I had waited long enough to join this army and that if I waited much longer the war would be over. Father served, you served, now it is my turn," exclaimed William with a slight sarcastic tone.

"Well, at least it sounds like you have stopped to think it over a little. I remember when you were inspired to just someday wear the uniform and carry a soldier's musket. You thought it would be exciting. Now God forbid, you will find out the other side of it too. How has Mary been?" asked Charles.

"She's been doing well. I am going to miss her lunches, though. Don't know how long I can eat these army victuals," laughed William.

Charles reached out his hand to shake his brother's hand and the two embraced and patted each other on the back. Then both brothers and their friends sat on several logs they had dragged over by their tents and talked until the wee hours of the night. It was a good chance for everyone to catch up on their hometowns and for some of the veterans to tell some stories too.

The next morning most of Bagley's Regiment was present at Fort William Henry so they were formed and reviewed by the colonel. After formation the men were told off for duties around the camp, as well as for guard duty and work details. Charles was sent to work on the ships being constructed. William's company was sent on a wood-cutting detail to the west of the fort. For days the two brothers worked around the fort, sometimes working on the wall around the entrenched camp, the ships and bateaux being built, other work details and general soldierly duties. William was getting a taste of what the majority of a soldier's life was like: work and boredom. The brothers were thankful, though, for the evenings that they got to spend talking and enjoying the closeness that their plights had brought them.

On August 1, Captain Learned of Colonel Ruggles's Massachusetts Regiment called for volunteers for a large scout General Winslow had ordered him on. They were to advance to the enemy advanced guard and reconnoiter. To Charles's surprise that night, William told him he had volunteered.

"I'm growing ill of the stench around this camp, all the sick, the garbage the soldiers litter the camp with, all the work details we spend our time on; work, work, work. That's all we ever do around here!" complained William.

"That is what most of a soldier's life is centered around," rebuffed Charles.

"Well, I am one that did not volunteer for this army to come all this way and build boats. I can do that at home and then sleep in my own bed in a house at night, instead of sharing a tent with six others."

"I tried to tell you that the life out here was nothing glamorous, but a lot of hard and dangerous work," said Charles.

"Speaking of danger, I am going to try my hand at some of that scouting that you wrote home about so much. I volunteered for that scout today that is heading up the lake tomorrow. The one with Captain Learned," exclaimed William.

"You what? You do not know the first thing about the woods around here, and the Indians. You've never been under fire. You need some training before you venture out and risk your life. Half of those men will be greenhorns like you, and you expect to learn scouting!" yelled Charles.

The two continued their arguing for about a half hour that evening and then Charles came to grips that William was now a soldier and if he volunteers for a duty, then he must follow through, and if there are consequences then he must suffer them himself and there was nothing he could do about it.

The next day Charles awoke early and went to Captain Learned's tent.

"Sir, I understand you have a sizable scout venturing out today. I would like to offer my assistance to you. I have been out on several scouts up the lake. Matter of fact the last one I was on went past Crown Point. I have often been out with Captain Rogers of New Hampshire. I can scout and if you do not have a clerk with you I can assist you with that sort of duty as well," offered Charles.

"Very good, Nurse. I have a little room left for some good men, men with skills that could be useful. I have many men marching with no experience. It would be helpful if you came with us. I have sixty of us now. Corporal, I have orders from General Winslow to travel to the French advanced guard and see what they are up to. If I can continue I am to take a look at the work being done on Carillon also. You have been to that area, correct?" asked Learned.

"Yes, Sir, I have several times," replied Charles.

"Alright Corporal. You can lead a squad for my detachment. Your men will be in the second boat," ordered the captain.

"May I request one man to be in my boat, Sir," asked Charles.

"Certainly."

"William Nurse, Sir, my brother," replied Charles. "It is his first scout, Sir and I'd like to be able to teach him a few things on his first time in enemy territory."

"You'll be having a chance to teach some things to several men, Corporal. Just see to it, it doesn't interfere with your duty," instructed Learned.

"Yes, Sir, I'll be ready and report just before sunset sir."

"Dismissed, Corporal," ordered Learned.

Charles went to work on the lighter at the wharf. Just after the evening roast beef he went to his barracks and collected his scouting gear and hurried to the wharf where most of the men had begun to collect. Just as he got there one of the lighters set sail and headed up the lake. He could see standing on her bow Captain Rogers. Charles could also see several familiar faces scurrying around the deck.

Within minutes, a gruff old sergeant stepped forward and barked some commands. "All right, you low-life farmers, get into a line here and present yourselves for the officers to give some orders," the sergeant shouted. The men jumped into a line. There were men from Connecticut and New York, but most were from Massachusetts.

Captain Learned stepped forward and stated, "Men, there are to be ten in each boat. Make sure that you keep together, not like a gaggle of geese but in a single line, like, like ducklings following their mother. You need to keep silence though as we progress, as the enemy will be expecting us to be moving in their direction. NCOs step forward." Charles and five others took a step forward. "You men divide the detachment up and get them into your boats," ordered Learned. Charles wasted no time in putting his brother in his boat. The look on William's face when he saw his brother was pure shock. And when he ordered him into his boat William could have killed him, but he did as told. In a short time all sixty men were in the boats and they had pushed off and were pulling their oars north up the lake. By daybreak they had rowed about fifteen miles. Learned's small flotilla came around a small peninsula and seeing the lighter that Captain Rogers' scout had anchored there, directed his men to land. They were given time to eat some cold victuals from their haversacks and the officers from both parties discussed their next move.

"Captain, I am not as acquainted with the areas north of here as you are and I am not sure of the abilities of my scout. Many of them are very new to this area, being fresh recruits," offered Learned.

"I intend to march my rangers the rest of the way. I think we can sneak in on Frenchy that way. I think if we continue any farther with the lighter we will be spotted. I am going to be marching not too far from their advanced guard. How about we join forces from here? A larger scouting force would not jeopardize either of our missions," answered Rogers.

"That sounds very appealing, Captain. I place myself under your command," stated Captain Learned.

In a very short time the two parties had combined and they were marching north along the ridge of mountains toward the French advanced guard and Carillon. Rogers knew Charles's capabilities so placed him and his ten-man squad of Massachusetts men on the left flank. The weather was hot and the insects ravenous. Every three hours Rogers stopped the march and the men took refreshment. Finally, that evening, when a halt was called it was estimated the scout was about one mile from the enemy advanced guard. Rogers called the officers and NCOs together.

"We are only a mile from our destination. I do not want to risk giving away our position by moving in the dark so I will take two rangers with me and reconnoiter the enemy position. The rest of you post a guard, half on duty, half get some rest. Captain Learned, you have command."

Rogers quickly gathered two other rangers and scurried out of sight. Captain Learned issued orders to the other men and they settled in for the night. Shortly before daybreak Rogers returned and began to awaken the troops.

"Alright, we are going to march to a vantage point we found last night. I expect strict silence on the march. Captain Learned you have the main body, Ensign Johnson you take five men for our rear guard, Sergeant McCurdy you have the right, Sergeant Moore you have the left. Nurse, Cunningham, Burbank and Henry you're on point with me," ordered Rogers. "Lets move out!"

The scout moved swiftly up the adjacent mountainside taking about an hour and a half to climb. Just before the edge of the summit Rogers raised his left hand and halted the column. The men in the point squad with him immediately dropped to one knee positioning themselves behind trees and rock outcrops. "Nurse, go back and get the Captain and six other men and get them up here quietly," whispered Rogers.

Charles backed out of the position and jogged down to the main body of the column.

"Sir," said Charles. Captain Rogers wants you and six others up top."

"Grab your men and lead the way corporal," instructed Learned.

Charles turned around and listed, "Nurse, Lowell, Bolton, Holt, Greenleaf, Nichols, with me." The Captain and the six men scampered up to the summit after Charles.

Rogers and the others had taken up positions and were lying prone peering down towards the water. He motioned for Captain Learned and the others to join him. Quietly they crawled up to the edge.

"Down there," pointed Rogers. "That is the advanced guard. See their tents and the movement around the edge of the woods," he whispered. "Wait a minute," he whispered. "Give me that glass," stated Rogers as he nudged Burbank. Rogers lifted the glass to his right eye and stared off in the distance across the lake. "On the other bank, at the old Indian carrying place. I see more of the enemy. They have split their guard up on each side of the lake."

Charles by this time had brought his brother up along the edge with most of the others. Charles whispered to William. "See where the Captain is looking? On the other bank, you can just make out where a crick is emptying into the lake. Just north of it if you watch you can see movement. Back in the woods I can just make out some glimpses of white, probably tents." William just lay there stretching his vision as far as he could.

"It looks to me to be about 200 on this shore and closer to 400 on the other," whispered Rogers to Learned.

The two officers crawled back below the summit and the others continued their vigilance. After a few moments, a sergeant was sent up to collect all the provincials just below the summit, but left the rangers on top.

"After deliberation with Captain Rogers we have decided that it is not prudent to linger here any longer and he recommends that if their advanced guard be this large that our provincials do not continue further. Mr. Rogers will continue with his smaller party, but we will fall back to Fort William Henry and report to the field command the situation of the advanced guard. Ready the men for the march," ordered Learned. "I want to be under way in five minutes.

And so, Captain Learned's party left for the south and Captain Rogers and his rangers headed farther north to view Carillon. The next morning William awoke with a terrible headache and chills. Charles knew how some camp diseases could quickly ravage a soldier on the frontier so he made William as comfortable as he could on the march. Within two days, they had arrived back at the fort. By this time it was recommended that William report to Henry Liddel, the regimental surgeon. Liddel could not tell immediately what was ailing William so he had Amos Putnam, his surgeon's mate, put William in his own tent and check on him through the next day. Charles was worried so went with them, but could not stay long before having to report for duty.

"William, you rest here and keep covered. Drink as much of this tonic as you can. I'll be back to check on you shortly," said Putnam.

Charles sat on the ground at the front of the tent and talked to William. "I told you not to come out here. I hope you are just ailing from something mild," offered Charles. "What did you think of your first scout?" asked Charles.

William was obviously tired, but attempted to carry on a conversation.

"I was impressed with how large Lake George is," said William.

"You should see Lake Champlain," replied Charles.

"Major Rogers and his men are everything you said in your letters. He is definitely one of the best woodsmen I have seen. He is every bit as good as Old Syrus the bear hunter back home. Is it true that he can smell Indians? That is what they say back home," asked William.

"I have never witnessed that, but he sure can find his way through the woods even in the dark," boasted Charles. "You'll get your chance yourself to see and smell as many Indians as you can only imagine. There will be many on our army's march north, and I have also heard that we will have a company in our camp too. Captain Burk tells me that there has been a company of thirty Stockbridge Indians who have been scouting around the Mohawk River and between Albany and Fort Edward. I understand that they came in to our fort three days ago with two French scalps. They raised quite a ruckus. Burk says that they are not dressed in English clothing like back in our colony, but rather are clothed mostly in Indian garb. They also are painting themselves and do not crop their hair. I expect this is to scare our enemy. Evidently, the generals are not sure what to do with them so they have assigned them to Rogers's ranging unit as a separate company," reported Charles.

William was starting to nod off now.

"I also have heard that the redcoat general plans on coming up to our fort almost any day now and maybe we can move on the enemy at Carillon before the summer is too late. We are finally getting our reinforcements, even if some are redcoats!"

Charles had to report for a work detail so he now had to leave William.

"I'll check on you tonight brother. Get some sleep and drink that tonic. You'll feel better before you know it," offered Charles.

Charles checked on William after work that day but he was still sleeping. After supper he went to the surgeon's quarters to see what they thought was ailing his brother. The surgeon was still not sure, but thought the fever would break by morning if it was nothing serious. Charles sat with his brother most of the night.

The next morning William awoke first. He took a sip of tonic, lay back down, and stared out the tent flap. Someone coming out of the tent next to William's knocked over a musket which fell onto a mess kettle and woke Charles with a start. He jumped to his feet and quickly looked around. Once finding his bearings he peeked into William's tent. Charles was terrified! He had seen it before, all too often here at the fort. Just as it had manifested with William: a fever, then headache and now the pox! William's face was covered with the round, flat, red rash! Charles hurried to the surgeon and Putnam and Otis, the other surgeon's mate carried William on a litter to one of the surgeon's tents, a quarantine spot for pox victims. Charles was forlorn.

AS FAR FROM HEAVEN

AS POSSIBLE

Charles's worst nightmare had come to be. His brother was amongst the men dying daily at the forts. Little could be done for the ravenous disease. He remained vigilant as much as the army allowed, but he was ordered to continue his duties.

Bagley's regiment was issued tools and began digging an entrenchment around the camp. Charles's company had a twenty-four foot section that they must dig and fortify. Part of the men, with Charles commanding, went to cut wood for fascines, but nothing could take his mind off his brother. It was not meant to be like this. William was not even supposed to come out to the war; he was too young. Charles had been very explicit on reasons not to join the army! In the evenings when he did not have guard duty, Charles would visit William in the surgeon's tent.

William had been suffering for nearly a week and Charles hurried over to the surgeon's tent just before dusk. He could smell the musky stench of sickness before even entering the quarantined area. With a lump in his throat, Charles entered the tent and walked over to his brother. William was asleep, taking large gasping breaths. Sweat was rolling down his face drenching the bedding under him. The disease had evolved to its final stages; high fever, excruciating headache and the red rash had developed into pus-filled, oozing soars. Charles knelt by his brother. He put his head in his left hand, and lowering it to his knee, he was silent.

After a few moments, he began to whisper.

"Lord, I do not understand why You have chosen to take my brother. He has always been faithful to You and he has always been true to his family. He is too young, Lord, to take him from us and he has so much to do yet in his life. Why did You allow him to come here to this place so far away from Heaven? You must have known that this would happen but You still allowed it."

Then William's eyes fluttered. He slowly turned his head toward Charles.

"Brother, you're here. Whom are you talking to?" asked William.

"No one, William. How are you this evening? It is beginning to rain outside so it should cool quickly tonight," reassured Charles.

"I am so warm, Charles. My head is pounding like John used to beat on his anvil with his sledge. I want to go home..."

Charles was at a loss for what to say. There was no way the surgeons were going to release William and there was no way he would survive the journey back to Amesbury.

"You need to sleep, William. You rest and I will sit here with you for a while. Maybe the cooling night rain will make you more comfortable."

William's head turned away and he seemed to fall instantly asleep again. Charles took out his journal, inkpot and quill and began to pen a letter home. He felt that he had better begin to break the news to his family.

My dear Mother and Father,

To my surprise, William arrived here several weeks ago. I had hoped that I had made my thoughts clear that he should not venture on this journey, but he, as well as you, must have deemed it feasible for him to enter into the service of our colony.

Shortly after arriving, William and I volunteered for a scout with Mr. Rogers. William obviously wanted to see if what I had written about my ventures was true. We accompanied a group of men north to the French Fort Carillon. After observing the enemy's advance guard, the officers decided that our party should head back to Fort William Henry to explain the situation while Captain Rogers and his party continued up Lake Champlain. On our way home, William took ill. When we arrived at the fort, he was placed in the surgeon's care. I had not written to you before this as I was hoping that he would improve. But alas, he has not and I feel it is best that I write you. William has contracted small pox. It has progressed continually and the surgeon tells me that the disease is in its final stages. He says that within the next day or two, William will dramatically begin recovery or he will pass into Jehovah's arms. I am sorry to have to bear such sorrowful tidings. I am at William's side now and he is resting.

A tear dropped from Charles's eye onto his paper. He attempted to wipe it away, but it smudged his last words.

It has been very difficult to concentrate on my work and I know there are many things happening around me, but I do not see many of them. I can tell you, Father, than General Winslow has been here and that there is a great ruckus amongst the field officers and most of the soldiery here about the idea of possibly serving with the regulars. Many officers will not serve if they are to be ranked below the lowest ranking regular captain.

There are many regulars now stationed at Fort Edward, but none yet here. They are passing through our cantonment though. Yesterday there was a group of highlanders and natives, about thirty heading north to scout Carillon. Daily there are small scouts of regulars, colonists and Indians leaving here or passing us to determine if the army will progress to attack. There are many reinforcements accumulating now. Even Captain Rogers' force has been augmented again. There is a group of Stockbridge Indians from our colony who have been placed into a company under his command. They have their own officers. Captain Jacob leads them. It is said that he is a town selectman of Stockbridge. Many of them are farmers back in Massachusetts, but they seem to have inbred instincts to follow sign and traverse the wilderness. They do not dress in clothing like we, as they do back home, but have adopted the native dress for their duties.

I cannot go on with droll trivia of camp life any longer. I cannot sit here and write you lightly about what happens around me with William lying here beside me, possibly taking his final breath. I must put down my pen and pray that Jehovah will take pity on our family and usher William from his deathbed.

I am sorry,
Your loving son,
Charles

Charles sent the letter with some dispatches the next morning. He went to his captain and got permission to stay with his brother. Knowing that it could be William's last hour the captain granted Charles's request. He went back to the surgeon's tent.

"He is not doing well," said Surgeon Liddel. He shook his head. "I am sorry, Charles, but I do not expect him to live through the night."

"I am just going to sit here with him. I talked to Captain Burk and he said that I could remain with William. I can only pray and continue to hope for his recovery," said Charles.

He pulled a chair to the side of William's cot. Pulling a book from his regimental he opened it and began to read to himself. He was reading from his Bible. After a few minutes he quit reading and lowered his head into his hands. This was more than he could stand.

The rest of the day Charles stayed by his brother's side. Periodically William would wake up and Charles would talk with him and give him something to drink. Around four in the afternoon William's body jerked and his eyes fluttered back in his head. Charles reached out to comfort William. Then William sat up in bed and immediately lay back down. His eyes were open wide and he was staring into space.

"Charles, are you there?"

"I'm right here, right beside you," said Charles rubbing his hand on William's shoulder.

Charles lifted William's head and gave him a sip of water. Then Charles gently laid him back down.

"I will be with you now," stated William.

"Who are you talking to?" asked Charles.

"Grandfather. He is here with me, can't you see him?"

Then a long, slow gasp of breath came from William. Then he closed his eyes and his head rolled to the side. He had passed away.

Charles pulled his hand back from William's body.

"Doctor Liddel, I think he is gone," Charles called urgently.

Liddel hurried over to the cot and checked William's body for signs of life. He held his hand up to his nose and mouth checking for breath signs and put his hand to William's left breast to check for the beating of his heart. Looking up at Charles and pulling the white blanket over William's head Liddel said in a very soft voice, "He has passed on, Charles. He is no longer in pain and he is with God now."

Charles was stunned. He could only sit there and stare at the body.

After about an hour Thomas, Gideon, and Joseph showed up. Liddel had sent for them, knowing Charles's state.

"Charles, you need to come with us," urged Thomas. "You need to come back to the barracks and we will have some food and we can talk."

Charles was silent.

Joseph put his hand on Charles's shoulder. "I know what you are going through. My brother passed last year."

They helped Charles to his feet and the four men walked slowly from the surgeon's tent and made their way to the barracks. The men put together some victuals, beef, rice, peas and butter. Gideon also brought a bottle from under his bunk. The men walked out of the fort and strolled over to the mess ovens. Joseph put some water into the mess kettle and mixed in the beef, rice, peas and butter and put the pot on the fire to boil. Thomas sat with Charles on the ground and Gideon took the bottle out of his haversack and offered it to Charles.

"Here Charles, take a drink, it may numb the pain some," offered Gideon.

Charles took the bottle and tipped it up and took a huge gulp. Each man in turn passed the bottle and also took a drink. Each time it got to Charles he took more than his share. Before too long the meal was done and the men filled their plates and began to eat. Charles could not bring himself to eat, though.

"Charles you need to eat," ordered Thomas. "You can't go without food. Eat some of your food."

Charles took one fork of meat and put the plate down and picked up the bottle again. He sat and took drink after drink. Thomas, Gideon and Joseph could only sit and watch. They figured the euphoria would only help Charles. It wasn't long and Charles had finished the rest of the bottle. That would have been fine but Charles thought he needed more. He stood up and announced, "Who's going with me? I am going over to the sutlers and get me some more rum. I need it!"

The three men got up and followed Charles. They passed the north end of the entrenched camp and started to see quite a few men congregating. Just the other side of them was a row of wall tents with flies attached to the front of the tents. These were the sutlers' tents. Charles and the others walked down the row of sutlers and Charles stopped at one of the first tents.

"Give me a gill of rum. I'm going to drink my way out of this hell!" ordered Charles.

The sutler that was standing behind a bench reached around and filled a gill mug and handed it to Charles.

"That'll be two pence, soldier."

"I'll get that one," said Thomas. He handed the sutler the coins.

Charles gulped the drink down and choked several times.

"What's wrong, can't stomach good rum?" laughed a rough-looking man who was standing at the edge of the bench.

Charles instantly threw a left jab directly into the man's nose. Blood splattered the man's face and everyone standing around him. Two of his friends jumped towards Charles and a scuffle ensued, but Thomas, Gideon and Joseph held them back. Charles ordered another drink but the sutler told him to move on.

Charles and his messmates moved down the row of sutlers. They were drawn in by some lively music being played at another sutlery.

"A round for my friends so we can drink to my brother," yelled Charles.

"What'll you have, mate?" asked the sutler.

"Why rum of course!" bellowed Charles.

"And what good fortune do we drink to your brother for?" questioned the sutler.

Charles's messmates froze, what would Charles do this time?

"To his death. He passed onto his Maker today," he replied.

"I apologize, mate, the drinks are on the house," stated the sutler.

"Then make it two, my friends here are thirsty," said Charles.

"No, Charles, one is enough for us," reassured Thomas.

"Then I'll drink 'em! Two for each, bar keep," slurred Charles. Charles and his messmates downed a gill each and Charles drank the seconds for Thomas and Gideon.

"My gratitude to you sir," said Charles as he dauft his hat. "We must be getting along."

Charles began to sway ever so slightly as he led the group farther down the sutlers row.

"Charles, don't you think we've done enough damage? Let's head back to the barracks and sleep it off," encouraged Joseph.

"I'm go'en no where's. If you want to go, you do so, I'm going down here," pointed Charles. Joseph and Gideon left but Thomas stayed with Charles.

Charles sauntered farther down the sutlers row. About three quarters of the way down the street, Thomas was distracted by some commotion in the Rhode Island camp. Charles selected just that time to also be distracted, but not by the same type of commotion. From his right Charles squinted his eyes and could see several women standing and sitting at a table under one of the sutler's flies of the Yorkers. He immediately was intrigued, and wiping his hand over his head so to flatten his hair, he stepped up to the table where the sutler stood. Charles bumped against one of the men, who quickly grabbed Charles by the shoulder.

"Watch where you're going there, you bastard," yelled the man as he pulled Charles away from the table.

Charles was just enough intoxicated now to not have the reflexes to fight back. But he lucked out.

"Nurse, you ruddy dog, it's me, McCurdy. How you been?"

"Charles took a step back and focused on Sergeant McCurdy and stated, "I am drinking to my brother. He just died of the pox."

"Sorry to hear that, Nurse, this is one of my new friends, Jacob Naunauphtaunk. We just call him Lieutenant Jacob. He's one of those Stockbridge Injans from over your ways," said McCurdy.

Charles looked at Jacob. He was dressed in a waistcoat with no shirt, a breechclout, leather leggings, Indian shoes and was painted red with his coal black hair hanging loosely down to his shoulders. Charles didn't say much but McCurdy pushed a mug of beer under his nose so he took it and drank. He started to lean on the table that was actually the sutler's bar. Looking back again at the women, who had drawn his attention to begin with, Charles noticed two of the women looking at him intently.

The two wenches sauntered over to Charles. One put her left arm over Charles's shoulder and around his neck and she began to twirl his hair around her finger. The other leaned into him and put her hand on Charles's stomach.

"Who are you, soldier?" asked the first woman.

"Charles," he hesitated.

"Haven't seen you around here. Where you from?" she inquired farther.

"I'm from Massachusetts," responded Charles.

The two continued to tease Charles. Charles reached out and took his mug from the bar and lifted it to his lips and the second wench whispered into Charles's ear, "Wouldn't you like to come with us? We have a more comfortable spot and some good West Indies rum. We can be comfortable and talk more privately."

"I guess so. West Indies rum huh?" replied Charles.

The two women began to pull Charles away from the bar. "Lets go. Come with us, Charles," whined the women.

The three left the sutler's tent and walked around behind the sutler's row and to a group of tents. Charles was staggering so much the two women had to partially guide him. One of the women lifted one of the tent flaps of the closest tent. "Come on in," she offered slyly.

The three entered the tent and they lowered Charles down on a pile of blankets. One sat down with him and began to rub his shoulder and leg.

"I'll get you some of that rum," stated the other.

"My name is Abigail and that is Katherine," offered the women fetching the rum.

Katherine was tall and slender with long flowing raven hair. She was dressed in a brown petticoat and a red bodice. Her hair framed her dark skin perfectly, which accentuated her high cheekbones. She appeared to be of mixed blood, Indian and English. Abigail had shoulder length blonde hair and had a pale complexion, but she had painted her face with light rouge on her cheeks and reddened her lips with a darker scarlet. She had begun to nibble on Charles's ear.

Katherine came over and sat down beside Charles and handed him a ceramic mug of rum. As he took it she took his other hand and put it around her shoulders and placed her head on his chest. Charles was stunned, but the drink was getting to him. He sipped the rum and then reached forward, placing it on the ground before him. When he sat back up Abigail was just pulling down her chemise exposing her voluptuous breasts. She immediately took Charles's hand the placed it on one of her breasts and began to kiss him. Katherine could feel how shocked he was so she slipped one of her hands under his shirt and began to massage his thighs. Charles could do nothing but give in to their caresses. His breathing began to race and the wenches began to lower him back onto the blankets. Charles felt helpless, but he knew that the drink had made him this way. Abigail pulled his shirt over his head and Katherine began to unbutton his breeches. Charles rolled his head back and Katherine began to kiss his face and his lips. Suddenly Charles could feel the soft lips of Abigail running down his chest to his stomach. He arched his back and moaned in delight. The three became lost in ecstasy.

There was a commotion in the street before the tent and the tent flap flew open!

"What the hell you doing, Nurse!" yelled McCurdy.

"We have to get him out of here!" urged Thomas.

The two men and Jacob the Stockbridge had come looking for Charles and were ready to save him from whatever fate awaited him. McCurdy reached forward, grabbed the tall wench by the arm, and dragged her from the tent kicking and screaming. Jacob pulled the other to the side as Thomas helped Charles to his feet. Thomas pulled Charles's shirt back on and scolded him. "Charles, button your breeches, we've got to get out of here now!"

Just at that moment, several men including the sutler from the bar came rushing around the corner of the sutler's tent and came toward them.

"Leave those women alone," ordered the sutler. "They are just working for me."

"You'd better back away, you ruddy bastards or the Adjutant will find out about your little business here and he'll shut your operation down and have you driven from camp! You'll never work at a military camp again!" warned McCurdy. "Do you want to lose all the business the rangers bring you, too?"

The sutler and his strong arms stepped aside and the other four men hurried away. Thomas and Jacob put Charles's arms around their necks and led him down the camp streets with McCurdy leading the way. They made it to the ranger camp and McCurdy ordered them to place Charles on the ground before a campfire.

"Jacob, pour him a mug of that coffee," said McCurdy as he pointed to a pot on the fire. Jacob did as ordered.

Thomas began to scold Charles. "What in the name of hell did you think you were doing? You know you don't drink like that. Those wenches are here in camp to make a living. They could have been just tempting you and then have men waiting to jump you, beat your brains in and steal your money!"

Charles took the coffee and drank. After about an hour he began to sober up and Thomas helped him back to his barracks. Charles was very embarrassed but even more, he had also began to remember what had driven him to do such terrible things. William. His grief for his brother weighed heavily on his mind and he lay in his bunk without ability to sleep. Lighting a candle Charles began to write to Mary, hoping to take some of his mind off his brother.

My dearest Mary,

I have been lax in my writing and apologize to you. I have been busy with scouting and with work duties. As I am sure you are aware, William came to join me in the army here at Ft. William Henry. I was very pleased and worried at the same time, and as I now know it the worrying was for naught.

I am so forlorned and miss you so much. William became ill shortly after arriving and has lasted only a few weeks. He has died of the pox. I do not know how I will make it any longer. I wish I could come home to you, or that you could come to me, but then again I do not want you here for if I was to lose another I may die.

When this fall comes and the army is sent home I have decided to come home to you. I will not spend another month in this God forsaken place! Men die all around me, five to six every day. I am so tired and I dread for my officers to ask any more of me, for I am afraid that I may say no to their orders.

I know I should not but I intend to enlist for another scout with the rangers in hopes that getting away from this camp will help me cope with my loss.

I pray that you will not torture yourself with the loss of my brother. I know how much he meant to you. Please try and fill yourself with the passionate anticipation of our uniting in the near future. I love you so and am coming home to you! When next I sleep I will dream of your arms around me once more.

Yours Affectionately,
Charles

At daybreak, Charles went to the surgeon's tent to make arrangements for William. William's body had already been moved to the cemetery. Charles hustled back to his regiment and reported to Captain Burk. He requested the rest of the day off to see to the burial of his brother. Burk agreed and Charles went back to the cemetery. Shortly after he arrived, two men showed up and began to dig graves. Charles stood by his brother and prayed. It didn't take long for the two men to finish several graves. Charles helped them then with William's burial. His body was wrapped in one of the white military blankets. It was marked with a red circle painted on it designating the body within as a pox victim. A chaplain from William's regiment had been detailed to attend the burial. He stood beside Charles and recited a Scripture and said a prayer. William's body was placed on two ropes that the men draped on the ground beside the grave. Then they lowered William into the grave using the ropes. Charles then stood at the foot of the grave, silent as the two men shoveled it full of dirt. After several hours Charles went back to his barracks and collected his quill, ink and some paper. He walked into the woods south of camp and sat down to write a letter.

Dear Mother and Father,

I regret having to bring you such news but I have no choice. William had arrived at camp and we went on a scout to the north. I was very surprised to see him arrive. As you, Father, know, when soldiers live in close quarters diseases can spread very quickly. The small pox had been one of the diseases infecting our soldiers here north of Albany. William contracted the disease. He first became ill on our return from our scout. Shortly after reporting to the regimental surgeon it was diagnosed. The disease moved quickly and I regret that yesterday he passed into Jehovah's hands.

I know how hard it is for me to deal with this loss and can only imagine the grief that you will feel. I ask you to remember that he was brave and only wanted to do his duty here like the rest of us. Please remember that he is in a better place now.

With my own personal grief I feel it may be best for me to advance with the first scout that heads north. I do not intend on throwing myself in harm's way, but find a need to divert my actions and thoughts as quickly as possible. I imagine that the army will not remain much longer this year so I should be returning to Amesbury shortly this fall.

Your loving son,
Charles

QUESTIONING DUTIES

Within weeks, a new scout had been arranged and Charles sought permission from his captain to volunteer. Captain Rogers was putting together a scout to the north. He was ready to vent some of his anger and grief and thought this was a chance to leave the boredom of camp. Charles's unit had been moved out into tents so he left his camp and marched over to the ranger camp. At Rogers' tent, Charles reported his business to a soldier posted.

"I'm here to see the captain. Corporal Nurse, of Colonel Bagley's Regiment. I thought to volunteer for his next scout. I've been with him on scouts before."

"Wait here, Corporal," responded the soldier. He entered the tent, and coming out again told Charles he could enter.

Rogers was standing in the side of the tent peering at a map that had been pinned on the wall of the tent. He turned to Charles and they returned salutes.

"So you want to go a-scouting again, Nurse?" questioned Rogers.

"Yes sir, I figured that it would be good for me to get out of here and I thought I'd offer my help to you. I hear that you are taking some of the redcoats this time, too," answered Charles.

"I've been ordered to start training some of them in rangering. I have got a handful of them and a like number of my men, too, going on this one. I can always use a good man. Have your gear ready to depart at sunset, at the third wharf," stated Rogers.

Charles readied himself, dressing in his ranger clothing and making sure he had his rations of food and ammunition. Just before sunset, he reported to the wharf. Men were starting to congregate and the veteran rangers were making sure they all had what was expected and that all was stowed away in the whaleboats. Charles reported to Noah Johnson, who was now a lieutenant. "Corporal Nurse, sir, reporting for scouting duty."

"Good to see you back with us, Nurse. Have you finally decided to join us for good now?" asked Johnson.

"No, I just figured it had been long enough that I had been cooped up here at the fort. I need to get out and see some different surroundings," replied Charles. "Looks like we have some different faces this time?"

"The captain is to teach some of these redcoats how he scouts. Over there," he pointed at the whaleboat, "that man in the bow is Hervey of the 44th, and beside him is Mr. Chalmer. He was sent by the quartermaster general just to learn what we do. And in the other, that's Captain James Abercrombie."

"Who, Abercrombie?"

"Yep, that's right, Abercrombie. He is the nephew of the general. We must be real privileged or someone really wants to keep an eye on us. Don't pay it no mind, Nurse, we're just here to do our job and this time one of our jobs is to show these fellers how to scout," stated Johnson.

"They seem like an honest lot. I look forward to serving with them," responded Charles.

"Stow away your gear and let's get ready to get under way, then," ordered Johnson.

Charles placed his knapsack, blanket and haversack in the boat and lightly tied his musket and cartridge box to one of the center gunwales of the boat. By this time the boat was filling up and Rogers himself came down to the wharf. Taking a few final glances at the men and boat, he turned around and nodded to an officer who had walked down with him. With a large gangly leap, Rogers bounded into the boat and gave his orders as he made his way to the bow.

"Make sure everything is tied in. Keep your mind on watching for the enemy at all times. Quiet from this point forward." Then he turned and ordered his brother Richard, "Let's push off." And Richard, who was last to leap in the boat, gave it a final shove and they were under way.

The men rowed through the night and the next day. Just before dusk it began to rain. About four miles south of where the French advanced guard had last been sighted Rogers ordered the whaleboat to shore on the east bank. Here they concealed the boat and Rogers pulled Richard, Chalmer, Hervey and Johnson together.

"I intend to move up past the enemy guard and reconnoiter the fort. I am taking Richard, Abercrombie, Gibbs, Nurse, Henry, Cunningham and Leiton. Chalmer, take Johnson, McNeil and the others with you in another party. Your orders are to find the enemy boats moving up the lake from the fort. Once your party has this intelligence you are to make haste back to Fort William Henry and report to the commandant. I will find what I can about Carillon and get us a prisoner. Then we will head back to the fort as well. Any questions?" demanded Rogers.

"Understood, Captain," replied Chalmer.

After a four-hour rest, the entire force got back in the whaleboat and quickly crossed the lake to the west shore. After concealing the boat the parties split and Rogers formed his seven men and marched north toward the French fort. By daybreak Rogers and his party were hidden about a half a mile from the fort. From this vantage point they could see that the enemy had been very busy. Not only were they working hard on the walls of the fort, but had built a large blockhouse by the southeast corner of the fort. The walls of the blockhouse had gun ports cut in them for cannon. A new battery had also been built east of the blockhouse to cover the lake. South of the fort there appeared to be five newly constructed houses near the water and Rogers counted twenty-seven bateaux on the beach before them. In the cleared plain southwest of the fort the rangers counted 160 tents. Lying in concealment they continued to observe the enemy the rest of the day.

After dark, Rogers left two men to watch the fort and moved the rest of his men farther from the enemy. The men paired up and half attempted to sleep while the others kept watchful eyes. Charles and Thomas Cunningham teamed up and found a fallen tree trunk for one of them to lean on and a thick soft carpet of moss for the other to use as a mattress. Thomas sat down and rested his back against the tree and Charles flopped down on the moss. After the last week he easily feel asleep.

Suddenly, Charles woke with a start, as did all the rest, hearing gunshots off in the distance. Rogers immediately dispatched Sergeant. Henry to see what was array. At dawn Rogers took Cunningham and they climbed to the falls between Lake George and Lake Champlain where the gunfire had come from. Henry met them part way and led them to a summit just before the falls where they took stock of a new fort being built by the French. Henry also reported that he had found the advanced guard from this new fort and that he thought that the guard was 500 men and there were equally as many at the new fort. With his observations complete and with new news about the area around the enemy fort, Rogers headed his troop back to the whaleboat. They waited till seven the next day in hiding to see if Chalmer and his party would show up. Judging that Chalmer had found the enemy boats and quickly marched for home, Rogers and his men climbed into their boat and rowed for Fort William Henry.

Upon return to the fort Charles was placed on work details helping to build the entrenchments and alternated work on the new wharf. The weather began to slowly make a change and the coolness of the early fall along with more frequent rain made the place even more dismal. Charles was still having trouble dealing with the loss of his brother. Always the hard-working soldier, his efforts had not gone without observation. He did not know it but Captain Burk and Robert Rogers had been making comments to some of the officers about

Charles's leadership and close to a week after his return, he was ordered to his company commander's tent.

"Come on in, Nurse," stated Burk.

"Yes, sir," replied Charles.

Charles stepped into the marquee and saluted the captain. Burk returned the salute without looking up. "A moment, Nurse," ordered Burk.

Burk and several of his officers were going over some orders and paperwork on a table before them. When they had finished Burk dismissed the other officers and turned his attention to Charles.

"Nurse, have a seat," offered Burk as he pointed to a chair.

Charles sat and removed his tricorn.

Burk began to speak as he shuffled some papers. "I wanted you to know how bad I felt about your brother passing away. That was bad luck, after just arriving here. I have been observing your work with the men who are placed under your squad and I have been kept informed about your duties when with the rangers. You have been a great benefit to your colony and your regiment these past two years. There are few that can say that they have done as much as you for the cause. I have also talked to the colonel and we have decided to offer you a sergeant's berth in my company. I think you have what it takes, Nurse. What do you say?"

Charles hesitated. "Captain, I have only done what was expected of me. No one else would have done less. I saw fit to volunteer at times and when needed I will always give my all. I would be honored to take the promotion, sir."

The two men shook hands, and Burk handed Charles a red sash with a white stripe in its middle. "This is your sash, Nurse. Wear it in honor and earn the respect of your men and they will follow you to hell if you ask it of them." The two saluted. "Sergeant, you are taking twenty men to Fort Edward with the next wagons heading south. You are to march as their guard and when you arrive, report to Colonel Meserve of New Hampshire. He is in charge of the men quartering on the island adjacent to the fort. You are to help him prepare the ground for more of the army's arrival and to assist in scouting details as needed. See my adjutant for your written orders. Dismissed."

Charles left the tent and as he walked to get his orders, he quickly wrapped his new badge of rank appropriately around his waist. After getting his orders he marched through the camp. When passing by the ranger camp, Noah Johnson, McCurdy and several others saw him and his new sash.

"Well, look what we have here, Lieutenant, a brand new sergeant!" spouted McCurdy.

"McCurdy, not in front of the camp," scoffed Johnson. "Nurse, how's it been going for you? I see your hard work has paid off. I wish you were one of my sergeants."

Charles walked over and shook their hands.

"Sergeant, let me introduce some of our new rangers, they're from your colony. This is Sergeant Moore, Sergeant Walter, Lieutenant Bulkeley and Sergeant Truett. This is the newly promoted Charles Nurse. He has served with us on several scouts now. The captain has tried to enlist him, but no luck yet." They exchanged salutes and handshakes.

"We have two new companies in our rangers now, Charles, Captain Hobbs from New Hampshire and Captain Speakman of Massachusetts. They raised men from your colony," stated Lieutenant Johnson.

"Most of them are from Boston, many from the docks. A rough, crude lot, but we are getting them ready to show those Frenchmen a thing or two. Most are used to fight'en," interjected Truett.

"I have to move on now. I've got orders to march for Fort Edward with the next wagons, so I must get my men ready," said Charles.

"From what I've heard, you'll be seeing some of us down there shortly. Watch your back, Sergeant, and stay away from those Yorker sutlers' wenches!" joked McCurdy.

Charles formed the twenty men under his detachment, inspected them for duty and awaited the movement of the wagons. About two in the afternoon the head wagoner told Charles he was ready to move his teams.

"Corporal Lowell, take the rear guard with Davis, Freeman, Osgood and Sweet. Shepard, Flag, English, Town, Fuller your on the right flank. Howard, McNab, Dunn, McCoy and Putnam, you have the left. I want it quiet on the march. Keep within eyeshot of the wagons. We'll march till dusk. I'll take the point. George, Merrill, Greenleaf and Noyes you are with me. Let's march!" ordered Charles.

Charles and his advanced guard jogged forward across the clearing to the road the entered the woods leading toward Fort Edward. They kept up their quick pace for about a quarter mile and then slowed. By this time they had placed themselves ahead of the wagons, but still just able to see them. In this fashion, they marched for five hours, and then called a halt. Charles placed half of his men on guard and placed them in a circle around the wagons. The rest of the men were allowed to eat and sleep. At about midnight the guard was changed and the rest of the party slept. At daybreak Charles woke his troops. He and Corporal Lowell had been up for about an hour and had made a walk around the perimeter of their camp to make sure the enemy was not to be found. The men ate a quick cold meal and began their march again. Shortly after leaving, it began to rain, which made the march most uncomfortable. Late in the afternoon, Charles's party came close to their destination. Rounding a bend in the road, a voice called out to Charles and his advance party.

"Who goes there?"

"Sergeant Nurse, of Bagley's Regiment. Coming from Fort William Henry with wagons," answered Charles.

"Come forward, Sergeant," was the reply.

Charles and his men moved forward slowly. Suddenly several men stepped out from behind a thicket. "Your orders, Sergeant," asked one of the men.

Charles pulled his written orders from his coat and handed them to the man.

"Very good, Sergeant. Captain Nathan Payson, of Lyman's Regiment. Welcome to Fort Edward. Corporal, lead the sergeant and his party to the fort," ordered Payson.

A soldier walked out from behind a tree and motioned for Charles and his men to follow him. They were led south and followed the trail between the fort and the river. At the west gate to the fort the wagons were halted and unloading began. Charles and his men were led then over the bridge onto the island just west of the fort. Much had changed since Charles had been there. On the island a group of a half dozen officers' huts and headquarters houses were about three quarters of the way up the island. At one of the houses Charles was brought in and introduced to Colonel Meserve.

"Sergeant Charles Nurse, sir, of Bagley's Regiment," stated Charles as he handed his orders to the colonel.

The colonel took a moment and read the papers. Meserve was a portly man with jet-black hair that was very gray around the temples. He had a very dark complexion, a very broad forehead and very pronounced features.

"Sergeant, to fill you in on the layout here on the island, let us step outside. The two men went out and stood beside Meserve's headquarters building and faced south.

"These buildings close by are officers' huts and headquarters buildings. The structures over there are huts for Putnam's Rangers." Meserve pointed to a small, double row of crude huts. "That is where your men need to put their tents." He then pointed to the cleared area with rows of white tents near the middle of the island.

"I see you have begun a sizable building beyond the camps. What is that to be?" asked Charles.

"That is to be a two-story blockhouse. I have been ordered to get it ready for other troops arriving soon," answered Meserve. "Have your men get settled today, and tomorrow they can start working on the blockhouse. You should report to the adjutant at seven tomorrow morning for written orders."

"Yes, sir," replied Charles.

Charles's detachment found a spot between the New Hampshire troops and the redcoats. This was the first time they had camped with the king's regulars. The regulars were the 48th Regiment of Foot, Colonel Burton's Regiment. After they were set up Charles and his men ventured about to get their bearings. One thing that impressed them greatly was how straight the regulars' tent streets were, every tent identical, stake-to-stake. That evening Charles's men had a hot meal, which felt good. It had gotten cold and a heavy frost covered the ground.

Early the next morning Charles reported to the adjutant's tent. Other sergeants and officers were also there to get their orders for the day. Details were ordered out to cut wood; several other work details were issued and three scouts of fifty men each were sent out in different directions under the commands of Major Miller, Captain Moore and Captain Hodges.

Charles and his men went to work on the blockhouse. It was to be a good-sized structure, about twenty feet square. The building was differing from many other buildings at the forts as it was made of stacking notched logs atop each other rather than posts and beams. The day passed quickly. The next morning Charles and his men were at work again on the blockhouse.

About two in the afternoon, there was a commotion on the west shore opposite the fort and island. A guard rushed from the northeast of the island into the woods. Shortly after, they emerged with a soldier. The guards brought the soldier onto the island and reported to Colonel Meserve.

The man was very battered, exhausted and appeared frightened. He was out of breath. There was blood running from a wound in his shoulder.

"Report, man," ordered Meserve. "Fetch him some rum and get Dr. Cutter, my surgeon, over here," spouted the colonel.

"Sir, I, I'm from Hodges's scout. Yesterday, we went out. To the west," the soldier pointed. "Indians and Frenchmen. They attacked our party. About ten miles out. They shot me and I went down. They kept coming, but did not see me. I made my escape shortly after, but I think they have killed the rest!"

The colonel turned to another officer beside him. "Major Saltonstal, muster 200 men and march immediately to the west. See if you can find them," ordered Meserve.

That night another man of Hodges's scout came in and then at about two in the morning three more arrived. The camp was alarmed twice in the night from these arrivals and at daybreak there was a call for volunteers to take one of Hodges's men out to find the spot of the ambush. Charles, Samuel Greenleaf, Joshua Merrill, Gideon Lowell, Jonathan Noyes and Ensign Samuel George volunteered. The Major formed his men for the march. George was give command of the right flank with Charles and the other four. After leaving the clearing around the fort the men were spread out. George moved his men about 100 yards away from the main body and had Charles place thirty-yard intervals between them. In this way they marched along the right-hand side of the detachment, always keeping a keen eye out for the enemy. Slowly they skulked through the woods. The soldier from Hodges's scout led them west, then cut north. They had made it a considerable distance when the entire group was halted. Four men scurried quickly from the advanced guard toward George and his right flank. It was a lieutenant and two men from Connecticut along with the man from Hodges's scout. They knelt down by George and Charles. Hodges's man pointed off to their right. "Over there. Can you see where the birch trees are clumped, near the cedar swamp? I think that's where they hit us." He turned around and pointed to a group of four large fallen pines. "I remember running to those trees and hiding for what felt like hours before I thought it was safe to move on."

"Ensign, take your men and check out that area. See if he is right," ordered the lieutenant.

"Sergeant, you take Greenleaf and Merrill and head along the south of those birch. I'll take Lowell and Noyes and head to the north," instructed George.

Charles wasted no time and had his men on the move, darting from tree to tree, attempting to keep as concealed as possible while moving as quickly as they could. They resembled a cross between a family of rabbits and a family of deer with the quick leaps and precision direction changes moving from cover to cover. It took about five minutes to get to the position they were pointed toward. Charles's group stopped quickly. They came across some gear, a haversack, a tumpline, then a canteen and a musket. Then, they slowly moved on, finding a shoe and then a coat. Looking up after picking up the coat, Charles's eyes caught the most hideous sight of his life! He thought he had seen carnage several times before, but this time he could not even move. Instantly, Samuel vomited beside him. Charles could feel his own body begin to shake. Before them were three four-foot poles and atop each pole was an impaled head! Such a gruesome sight of the grotesque contortioned expressions on the heads mixed with the dried blood and the mutilation from the killers and scavenging animals and birds! One head he recognized as that of Captain Hodges's. Finally, Charles could make his voice sound.

"Ensign George, over here," he strained.

George and his men moved toward the location and were horrified.

"Lowell, go back and tell them we found them, what is left of them," said George in a stunned voice.

"Over here," motioned Noyes. "Here are some bodies too."

About twenty yards behind the heads lay ten mutilated corpses. The bodies were hacked and bludgeoned. They barely resembled the men they once were. Charles fell to his knees and could only stare. What form of man could do such things? All the men could only stare. When the others showed up Charles took his men and formed a flank to protect a party who collected the corpses and heads for transport back to the fort. Before the work was complete Major Saltonstal's entire party was stunned and sickened by what they saw. Pulling them together they formed to march back to Fort Edward. Men were placed with care for safety on the march and within several hours they had covered the ten miles back to the fort.

When they returned to camp and were dismissed Charles and most of the men headed back to their tents. They noticed that more regulars and some more provincial troops had arrived. Charles and his men were taken off duty for the rest of the day. A new side of Charles had shown its self back at Fort William Henry; the war and its carnage had taken its toll. Charles pulled a bottle of Madeira wine from his tent, sat down and drank it as quickly as he could. Shortly after, he went to one of the sutlers and consumed several mugs of beer. Then he purchased a bottle of rum and walked to the southern tip of the island. No building or work was being done here so he had peace and quiet. He sat there in his own sorrow till dark, and eventually passed out. Around ten, that evening, partially sobered up, he walked back to his tent, lay down and fell sound asleep. His service had reached its lowest experience. He had lost his brother and witnessed the worst man could do to his fellow man. Was there still a meaning to his service for his country, for his colony, for his God?

THE END DRAWS NEAR

In the morning Charles awoke on time but with a drumming headache and a sick stomach. He pushed himself to get ready for he had duties he must attend to, being a new sergeant. He wolfed down some bread and cheese, drank some cider and hurried to the adjutant's hut for orders. Others had collected by the time he arrived but he did make it on time. He was pushing his luck and if he did not curb his actions they would come back and bite him.

Daily, orders were given and Charles took his men to work on the blockhouse. They had raised the walls of the first floor and were working on laying some logs across the walls to support the second story. This had to be done, for the second story was to overhang the first by two feet all around. The work was hard and the weather fair. At mid-day they stopped for a quick meal and at about four in the afternoon they stopped for the evening roast beef. After the meal, Charles would either return to his bottle, walk about in sorrow, or visit the sutlers' tents. This is the routine he fell into. The only variance was when his men also drew guard duty at night. In those cases Charles was smart enough to stay out of the bottle.

For several weeks the boredom of camp took its toll on Charles and his men and the sickness of the camp took its toll on many within the cantonment of Fort Edward. Daily it seemed that more than a dozen were falling ill from different camp distempers, the bloody flux or the dreaded pox. At the same time the camp was growing by leaps and bounds. Daily differing units of regulars and provincials poured into Fort Edward. Rogers and his rangers also arrived. The Stockbridge Indians, Rogers' own company and his brother Richard's company were told to make it their home. They were to make the island their headquarters and three detachments, of an officer and twenty men were to range daily in the direction of Wood Creek, South Bay and Ticonderoga. Meserve gave them the blockhouse for their quarters, but it was not to their liking so Rogers had his men begin to construct temporary huts between the officers and the tented area of the island. This meant that the area where Putnam had his men would expand dramatically. Before long there were rows of ten by ten foot lean-to style huts filled with rangers.

One of the most exciting days came on September 25. Charles and his men had been working on an entrenchment near the west side of the island. A halt was called on the work and before long the regulars were called into formation. Many of the officers were also forming up both on the south end of the fort and on the island as well. Then from a distance, Charles started to hear a muffled drum. He and his compatriots brushed it off as more recruits arriving. Then there was a faint wailing. It appeared to be coming from the road south of the fort. Charles and his men quickly moved over to the east side of the island. From their vantage, just south of the bridge, they could see the road leading toward the fort, the necessary houses, the new barracks buildings, the commissary and artillery stores rooms and the ovens. Any troops arriving from the south marched past this area and over the southern bridge either into the fort or around the west side between the fort and river. The sounds began to crescendo.

Alexander McCoy nudged McNab and spoke in his heavy Scottish brogue, "'Tis the most beautiful music from heaven. I remember from the time I was a wee lad in the old country, 'tis the pipes."

"Aye, the music from them I have heard my grandfather talk of. It must be a grand parade arriving to have such fine music," replied McNab.

Suddenly, from the edge of the woods, a group of rangers came into view. Then a smart-stepping company of King's Grenadiers, followed by a magnificent pair of silk flags emerged. The men next in the procession were mounted officers. There must have been twenty of them. Several of them were obviously high ranking. One of them Charles imagined was Lord Loudoun, the commander of the army. Their horses were draped with velvet blankets with sparkling gold trim that matched their riders' uniforms. They passed quickly, and then the drums and pipes entered the clearing and their music began to echo off the trees. Two ensigns followed carrying flags. The flag on the right was a king's colors and the flag on the left a buff colored silk with a canton of the royal flag. In the center, a crest could just be made out. A single mounted officer led a full regiment of troops. The soldiers were clad in redcoats, obviously the king's troops, but were accoutered differently otherwise. After the procession had stopped at the fort, this regiment was marched onto the bridge leading to the island. As the troops stepped down onto the island, Charles and his men could see that they were Highland troops, soldiers of the 42nd Regiment of Foot, Colonel Grant's Regiment. They were dressed from head to toe in the clothing of their ancestors. Atop their heads they wore a navy Scottish bonnet with a red woolen ornamental ball and headband. Their coats were red, faced buff and cut short resembling a doublet from the previous century. This was to accommodate the many yards of fabric from their kilts. Each man donned his great kilt, the king's plaid, a mixture of green, blue and black. Their hose were a red and white harlequin pattern.

As the Highland troops came onto the main parade on the island they wheeled to the left and when they had all aligned they called a halt. At the end of the line of march was a group of women and children, followers of the regiment. They quickly scurried to the rear of their regiment so as not to interrupt their soldiers' formation. Many of the followers were obviously wives and children of the troops. The men were then given orders to face to the left, bringing them front to their colonel. These were well-trained, battle-hardened troops. It took little time and orders were given and they had commenced their camp set up. Shortly after this the rest of the men in camp returned to their work as well.

The fort and camp around Fort Edward was filling up. But being late in September the weather was starting to close in. It was colder and it rained often, making it uncomfortable. Men were on constant work details, rations were running low, sickness was becoming rampant and desertions were increasing. General Loudoun with an escort of 500 of his regulars headed to Fort William Henry and north to scout the enemy.

Deserters were brought in from the Connecticut colony, fifty of them, and others as well from the regulars. There were also French deserters making it all the way south to Fort Edward. One group of fifteen were brought in, their army was beginning to suffer greatly, hundreds starving to death.

Along with the provincial and regular reinforcements arriving daily at the fort, natives started showing up. This lent greatly to the diversity of men in the camps. George Croghan came to Fort Edward with 69 Indians late in September. Two weeks later twenty Mohawks and Stockbridge Indians came in. Sir William Johnson, Secretary of Indian Affairs, also arrived at the fort with 63 Indians that were loyal.

The majority of the friendly natives were used for scouting. They took kindly to the Highland troops and many scouts consisting of Indians and Highlanders began to venture north. Many of the Indians evidently saw these men from Scotland as a form of Indians themselves. This may have been because of their dress; it may have been because of their rugged subsistence in the wilderness.

As the month wore on, things continued to change around the camp. The work was hard and the weather got cold enough to see some snow flakes. Rain came often. Charles had developed a reputation still for working hard, but also for drinking as well. This was rare for men from his unit. He ventured to the sutlers one night and was in the spirits. Joseph English and Alexander McCoy had gone with him this particular night.

"I am so damned sick of this place!" complained Charles. "I have been here working like a slave going on two years now and I am not going to stay much longer. I am sick of the stench, the death and dying, the work from sun up to sun down. Now we don't even get our damned rum ration regularly!"

"Quit your bitching, Sergeant, and have another drink. You have plenty to drink tonight, as long as the sutlers don't run out, or you run out of money," spouted McCoy.

"I've got enough coin on me to keep drunk for a month, if I need to," replied Charles.

"We are bound to be heading home soon. They can't expect us to attack the French in the winter, can they?" added English.

"You bastards have not been through everything that I have and you haven't seen some of the bloody, stupid orders that I have seen some of these officers give. You just do what I tell you and you will live to see home again," said Charles gruffly.

The three continued to drink but neither English or McCoy were keeping up with their sergeant. Then Charles began to spout off again.

"I am sick of fighting here in this stinking colony."

The three continued crawling into their stupor until Joseph coaxed his friends to call it a night. Charles agreed, as they had to be ready to do their duty in the morning. Little did Charles know but at the other end of the bar stood several Yorkers who were listening. Charles, Joseph and Alexander gulped their last mouthfuls of drink and started to walk away. Charles headed for the privy and told the others he would be back at camp shortly. He thought to himself it was too far of a walk so he turned around and walked over to the edge of the river to relieve himself. He began to unbutton his britches and he was struck in the back of the neck with a piece of wood! Charles staggered and fell to his knees. Before he could stand another man had jumped on him and pulled him the rest of the way to the ground. Charles was able to roll on top of his assailant and raised up to smack him in the face when the man who struck him with the wood kicked him in the ribs. Charles groaned and was shoved off the other. Immediately the two men grabbed Charles and lifted him to his feet. They held his arms tightly and from the edge of the darkness, a third man appeared. He walked directly toward Charles and began to slug him in the stomach and then in the face. Charles fought as much as he could, kicking the two men and attempting to pull loose. Blood began to flow from an open wound on Charles's head and his sight was instantly blurred. "So you have coin, do you? Give it to me or I'll beat the hell out of you!" warned the third man.

Then he hit Charles directly in the nose and Charles's knees became rubber. Charles still was not going to relinquish his money. One of the others kicked Charles in the stomach and the beatings started again.

A man yelled from behind the sutlers' tents and six men rushed toward the ruckus. "Stop! Get them!" McCoy had also not headed directly to camp and heard the commotion and quickly acquired the help of Corporal Lowell and a few others close by. By the time they had reached Charles the three attackers had dropped Charles in his own blood and had escaped into the darkness at the north of the island.

Charles was a mess. He now was unconscious. His friends helped him back to his tent and attempted to clean him up. The corporal did not think he was hurt badly enough to take to the surgeon and they did not want a report of Charles's drunkenness being brought before the adjutant either, so they let him sleep it off.

The next morning Gideon woke Charles early. "You all right, Charles?" he asked.

"My God. Oh, my head," groaned Charles. He attempted to sit up. He gasped and pushed on his ribs. "Who beat the hell out of me?"

"You don't remember?" asked Gideon.

"I don't remember much," whispered Charles.

"You went on one of your drunken binges and three men jumped you. English and McCoy said you were griping a lot and boasting that you had money. They were probably going to rob you," told Gideon. "Are you going to be able to report for duty?" he questioned.

Charles slowly sat up. He started to get to his feet. Gideon reached out and helped Charles. He sighed loudly and moaned. Then he put his hand on his head to feel for cuts and blood.

"I'm up. I think I can make it. Let me clean up," answered Charles.

"I'll walk with you for orders today," offered Gideon.

Charles poured some water from his canteen into a rag and washed his face and hands. Then he took a long drink and spit part of the water out. Holding his head down Charles then poured the rest of his canteen over his head. He stood up and shook his head like a wet dog, which sent pains through his head and body again. Putting on his uniform he took his haversack and walked with the corporal to the adjutant's tent.

Charles was really dragging. When they got there a few others had already arrived. McCurdy was there to get his orders for his rangers.

"Christ, Nurse, what the hell happened to you?" bellowed McCurdy. "Did you get run over by one of those 18 pounders?"

Charles looked up at him and stared for a moment and then answered. "I really don't need it today. I would rather not say."

Charles received many looks from the other NCOs and officers receiving orders. As soon as they could Charles and Lowell left the group and walked toward their camp.

"I did it this time," admitted Charles. "I can't keep doing this."

"You can't feel sorry for yourself forever, you'll destroy yourself," replied Gideon.

"I know. That will be my last drink for a while. If I can only make it through today," winced Charles.

They limped back to camp and gave out the orders to their man. Charles wasn't worth much all day but his men did what they could to cover for him. After the evening roast beef Charles took out his quill, ink and some paper and wrote to Mary.

My Dearest Mary,

I have reached the lowest degree of condition here at the war. I have ignored my duty to my men and shamed myself in their eyes. I have grown to hate it here and yearn for the day I return to my beloved Amesbury. You cannot know how much I need to come home to you. Will you still be waiting for me?

This place is filled with sickness, death and depravity. It is so much worse than you remember that I wish that no other relative of mine shall ever endure such harsh treatment or drift so far from God's will.

We have had many men from all the colonies arriving here daily. We now also have many redcoats amongst us. They are not a bad lot; many seem to be just like our men from the colonies. There are some that are dregs of society, but one must expect that when so many are brought together.

The weather here is getting cold and for several days there has been snow in the air. Today twenty wagons arrived from our colony with clothing for our men. I pray that we will not need them; that we will be sent home before it is too cold. I cannot imagine that our general will still want us to advance against the enemy this late in the season.

When I get home I intend to rest for a month. I am so tired and so in need of your care and comfort. I have been stationed back at Fort Edward now for near a month. You would not believe how much it has changed. Fort William Henry now is virtually complete to the plans the colonel showed me. When I left, they were finishing the final barracks. Despite the hell of this place, I have made many new friends, but I wish

*to be back at home with those friends more than you can imagine. I
must see my family soon. Above all, I desire to hold you again.*

Yours affectionately,
Charles

      The general had returned to the fort and called his officers
together. The meeting was held on the island under a large marquee.
Charles and six of his men were part of a large guard placed on the
tent. He could hear much of what was said. The commander, Lord
Loudoun, stood to address his military family. He was a short man, in
his fifties. He appeared a strong man, a man of military stock. His
hair had grayed and he wore it short on top, curled on the sides with
his queue in a black linen hair bag. His uniform was that of a warrior-
statesman. It was scarlet wool, of a very fine quality. He had adorned
it with a double row of gold lace with a golden aquillet on his right
shoulder. Over his right shoulder, he wore a silk sash as well. His
small clothes were equally lush and his waistcoat was laced in gold
patterns of zigzags. He spoke with a mild Highland accent.
      "I have approached the enemy lines myself, venturing north from
Fort William Henry. From this and other reconnaissance, and from
captured enemy deserters it appears that the French are suffering and
that they are due to head for winter quarters soon. I do not see it
prudent to advance at this late stage in the campaign. The weather is
changing and from what the New York officers tell me, we are not far
from having too much snow and ice to move our artillery. We have
labored too long at moving troops, equipment and supplies to this
God-forsaken part of the world. It is my opinion gentlemen, that we
hold here until I have word that the enemy has left for their northern
cities and then we too will place most of our troops in winter quarters
in Albany. Therefore, my orders are to prepare the army for winter
quarters, to move on my command. It is my wish that six companies
of Rangers stay under the command of Mr. Rogers, two companies to
be posted at Fort William Henry and four at Fort Edward. Mr.
Rogers is to use the island at Fort Edward as his headquarters. The
44th Regiment of Foot is to winter garrison Fort William Henry with
400 of their men. At Fort Edward, I intend the 48th Regiment of Foot
to leave 500 troops. The 42nd Regiment is to garrison Schenectady.
The remainders of the king's troops are to be quartered in Albany and
the provincials are to march for their colonies on my order. Are there
any questions?" The general hesitated momentarily. "Very well then,

you are dismissed to make final details and to ready the forts for winter garrison," demanded Loudoun.

That evening Charles again relaxed in writing a letter.

Dearest Mother and Father,

There has been so much happening here since I last wrote you. Not all has been good, but I find it difficult to spend my time now on dwelling on the parts of life here at the front that do not meet with God's keeping of His soldier's in arms against His enemies. We have been a very vain and procrastinating army. There are many aspects of our being here that are not worthy, nor meaningful to place into words, so I will give you only I hope, the betterment of our cause.

I moved down to Fort Edward near a month ago with a small troop of the men from my regiment. I was made a sergeant and given orders to march hence and to assist in preparations for more men to come. We have had hundreds of troops coming in daily. This is now a huge army, sitting, awaiting the orders of our new general. Lord Loudoun arrived here several weeks ago and brought with him several regular regiments. We already had several helping us garrison both forts for months. In place here are men from all our colonies and regulars of the 42nd, 44th, 48th, and rangers from various colonies as well. Here at Fort Edward, things have changed a lot from when I first described it to you. If coming from the south one sees the hospital and ovens, then the necessary houses. A bridge then leads over a crick, where there is now a barracks that some rangers will be staying in. There is also a storehouse there for the artillery. When entering the south fort gate there is a 30x75 barracks for the commandant and part of his staff. If you look to the east there is a large barracks for 300 men. On the west, there is another barracks for 200 men and a hospital for 100. There is also a casemate on the west that will house another 250 soldiers. Both the northwest and southeast bastions have powder magazines. On each side of the north gate there are two-story houses. The one on the right has four rooms and the one on the left two. It would be a splendid fort in its own, but there are expansions being made to the overall fortified area by adding a bridge to the west onto the island. The island is now home to many troops. There are officers and sutler houses, huts for various ranger units and a large tent camp. We have almost completed a sizable two-story blockhouse as well. Colonel Meserve of New Hampshire commands on the island and has planned entrenchments to defend the island.

I have spent much of my time this campaign with the rangers. I have told you before about Captain Rogers. It is very hard service, but also very gratifying. The high command has even started to send some of their officers out with him and his men to learn how his men scout. He recently has come back from a scout and I must tell you about it. He was ordered to scout the area of Ticonderoga. The enemy is building there and has accumulated a large army. Two soldiers were found posted outside of the fort. Rogers and five of his men crept close and had been observing the fort. The captain deemed it necessary to capture one of the enemy. One of the Frenchmen who were outside the fort was posted on the road leading into the woods. Rogers and his five men marched directly down the road in the middle of the day until the man challenged them. Rogers answered in French saying friends. The sentry was deceived until Rogers and his men came very close. Seeing that he was being deceived he yelled out, "Qui est vous?" Rogers answered, "Rogers!" The captain rushed forward and disarmed the man, then reaching around behind his back he pulled his scalping knife and cut away the man's coat and breeches, grabbed him by the hair and dragged him on the run behind him. Once in the woods, the Frenchman's hands were tied and a rope was placed about his neck to keep him from escaping. Rogers, his men and the captive then made haste back to the forts. When asked why he cut off the man's clothes Rogers said he did it so the man could keep up with them.

Our weather has been changing and the fall rains have been often. Snow has just begun and I wish I were home where the warm hearth was there to welcome me in each cold winter night. I have just heard, that we will be disbanding with in days and returning to our homes. The day I pray will come soon!

We have had some problems lately with having enough food. We are promised an issue of victuals but often we have not received them. Today we began to receive the King's allowance. We received our full allotment of salt beef, rice, peas, butter, flower and rum. It has been some time since we had all foodstuffs at one time!

The night is becoming cold and my hands are getting numb. I must complete my letter and warm myself by the fire for a short time before I lay down for the night. I hope that we march home shortly.

Your Loving son,
Charles

The next two weeks, final building was done on the fort to make preparations for the winter. Troops and wagons were on the road between Fort William Henry and Fort Edward daily. Stores were being distributed, bateaux were being moved for winter storage and troops were being concentrated at Fort Edward. Finally, on

November 11 the orders came to march for home! This had been a long time coming and Charles was elated. The army was to march off in two divisions. The colonels drew lots to see who went first and Bagley drew to leave the twelfth. At seven in the morning, Charles called his men to march to the parade. Once on the parade the entire regiment was formed along with the other regiments or parts that were to march under Colonel Bagley. Bateaux were placed on wagons and carts to carry the sick, lame and equipment. The air was crisp and a snow lightly covered the low spots on the ground. Finally, the colonel gave the orders.

"Major, have the division formed in columns of six and let's march," said Bagley.

Major Mathews saluted the colonel and turned about face to the formed army. The field officers mounted their horses and rode toward the bridge. Mathews's voice echoed. "Take care! Form lines into columns of six, by the left, wheel!" The men smartly moved as ordered. "Rangers take the point! To the front, March!" The rangers jogged over the bridge followed by the mounted officers and the troops stepped off after them. In this fashion followed by the wagons and carts filled with equipment, gear and the sick and lame, the army marched past Fort Edward, into the woods south of the fort and onward toward home.

COMFORT AND FAMILY,

HOME AT LAST

Bagley's division marched the entire day and arrived at Fort Miller around dusk. Fort Miller was a small stockade outpost used for a supply depot. The next day, they marched to Saratoga, arriving in late morning and by evening the division made it to Still Water. The men were in high spirits despite the hard march. The baggage had been transferred to a scow and the men were ordered to get only what they needed for the evening from it. Most of the men carried their essentials, a bedroll, axe and their mess kettle. Bagley's Regiment was ordered to make camp in the woods. Tents were not unpacked but rather the men made do with their bedrolls. Fires were kindled and the men warmed themselves as they prepared the evening meal.

Charles and his squad were ordered to assist the carters. The carters needed hay for their oxen so Mr. Waldo, the head carter, went to the fort to see if there was any to get. He came back shortly with news that there was none to be had. Samuel Greenleaf spoke up. "I saw some in the little barn, just east of the fort. There were no animals using it and it appeared to be a stockpile for feed."

"Sergeant, can your men take that cart and help a couple of my carters get some of that?" asked Waldo.

"I'll see to it," answered Charles. "Greenleaf, take six men and fetch a cart of hay from that barn."

In no time, Samuel and his detachment had marched the half-mile to the fort and barn where he had seen the hay. There was no guard on the barn so Samuel opened the doors and the carters filled their cart with what they needed and drove the cart back to the woods where the regiment was camped.

It was not long, and a squad of regulars marched up towards their camp demanding that they were under orders to confiscate the carts.

"You, carters, those carts are now king's property!" ordered the regular lieutenant in charge of the squad. "I'm bringing your carts back to the fort! You had no right to steal that hay!"

Then, the captain of the fort garrison showed up with another detachment.

"You heard the lieutenant. Arrest them, damn it!" the captain ordered the lieutenant.

The lieutenant took his squad and attempted to force the carters to harness up their oxen and march to the fort. Hearing the ruckus, Lieutenant Colonel Kingsbury, Bagley's second, came over and stopped the regulars.

"Stop that, who do you think you are? Take your hands off those men! What is the problem here, Captain?" asked Kingsbury.

"These men stole that hay and I am under orders to see to it that it gets back with the pilferers immediately," he answered.

"We had permission from the colonel to get what we needed. You had a whole barn of it! We were lied to. They said there was no hay! That was a bloody lie," stated Waldo angrily.

"I will be damned if dirty provincials are going to steal from the king!" yelled the captain.

By this time, soldiers were beginning to congregate around the carters' camp. Kingsbury, seeing the gravity of the situation, offered to give the hay back.

"Captain, you may take the hay back with you. I apologize for the misunderstanding, but you will not place these men under guard. You have your men take their bloody hands off them! They are not your prisoners!"

"This is a direct infraction of the king's laws and military law! I will have justice!" bellowed the captain.

"I fully understand that there has been a mistake made, but you are not the judge advocate and I will not have you misusing these men! I insist that you go back and work this out with the commandant or we are going to have severe problems!" demanded Kingsbury.

"You will be sorry!" boasted the captain. "Sergeant, take the damned hay back to the fort." The captain and his detachment of regulars confiscated the hay and angrily marched off. Thinking the episode done, most went back to their camps. Charles and his men went back to their fire where their meal was almost ready.

Suddenly, drums began to beat at the fort. Charles began to wonder if they were under attack! The men moved to the edge of the clearing to see if they could make out what was going on. Within minutes, they could see that the captain had formed his company of regulars and was marching them directly toward the provincial camp. Meanwhile, the lieutenant and his original detachment were attempting again to arrest the carters. Seeing this, Colonel Bagley quickly gave orders for his officers to form the entire regiment. The men acted quickly, they had been at war now for a year and some of them two. Once formed, the colonel had them encircle the carts, carters and the lieutenant and his regulars, and face out with their bayonets fixed!

"You are to let no man in or out of this circle except our own! That includes that damned lieutenant and his men! I do not care if they are the king's regulars or not!" ordered Bagley. "Captain Young, you have command!" yelled Bagley. Then Bagley and some of the other officers and Mr. Waldo hurried to the fort to see what could be done to resolve the issue. He did not want this to come to blows or worse yet, death!

Shortly after, the captain and his regulars came close. They marched to within eight or ten rods. The tension was great; would the provincials run? Would the regulars attack?

"Steady men, steady! They are our allies, there will be no fight here, just hold your ground!" urged Young as the regulars approached.

The regulars halted. Their captain marched closer and in a gruff voice asked, "Who is in command here?"

"I am, Captain Young," he answered. "What is your will?"

"I am here with my company to take the carts and carters!" demanded the officer. "You have my men also prisoners and I insist you release them! They are the king's troops and I'll have you beaten if they are harmed!"

"If you or any of your men come any closer, it will be at your peril! I have my orders and they are that no one shall come within my formation! And no one is leaving it either, until my colonel returns!" stated Young with stern authority.

It was a standoff! Neither side budged. Would the regulars attempt to push their way in, would they fire on them? Would Bagley's men hold their ground, would they give way and let the king's regulars enter their circle? After a few moments of extreme tension, the regular captain faced his men about and marched them back toward the fort in disgust. The provincials had been trained to follow directions and they stood their ground sufficiently to tell the regulars, they meant business. Shortly after, the colonel and the others returned from the fort. Somehow, the colonel had resolved the issue with the commandant. He assured the men there would be no more problems tonight. The lieutenant and his regulars were released and they quickly marched back to the fort. The men returned to their fires, ate their meal and after lively talk about the fire settled down for a good night's rest.

Early the next morning, the regiment was formed and marched south and arrived at Half Moon before night. It was the Sabbath, so the colonel ordered all to attend the chaplain. Then on Monday, they marched to Greenbush and camped in the woods. The next day, they reached Albany. Here, part of the units of the army deviated their march, heading for different colonies.

The men's spirits were high, but the march was belaboring after a hard year of work and campaigning. They walked east now through Kinderhook and Sheffield, over the Connecticut River and through Springfield. All along the way, men slept in fields or barns. The weather was crisp and rain fell often. Their feet were beginning to suffer.

Charles was ready to get home. It had been two years and he needed time to take stock of his life and recuperate. The regiment continued its march through Brookfield, Southborough, Sudbury, and Cambridge. By now, the men were beginning to drop out as they arrived or passed their hometowns. Once they had arrived at Boston, about one-quarter had left and now as they marched through the city, another large group headed for home. Charles and his friends did not seem as awed with Boston as they had been before. Their minds now were on arriving home in less than two days. They did not stop that night but continued their march to the north and by the next morning, the terrain began to look like home.

The regiment marched into Newberry. Lieutenant Colonel Kingsbury was left in charge of the men from town. Just under half of the men left were dismissed here. The colonel continued with the rest of the men.

They marched along the road parallel with the Merrimac River. In less than two hours, they had made it to just outside Amesbury. Suddenly, they were marching past farmhouses and small family groups were at the road's edge greeting them. Coming by his own home, Charles felt his heart swelled in his chest. He had made it home! Then came his parent's homestead. Charles could not believe his eyes; his family, Mary and her mother were all waving and cheering at the lane to the house. Periodically, men had broken ranks and ran to their loved ones but most remained in their ranks, making a point of staying with their regiment until a halt was called. Charles fought himself to do the same. They continued their march and turned up the road to the north, leading to town at the conjecture of the Merrimac and the Powow Rivers. Families had fallen in behind the regiment walking and riding, praying for the time that the regiment would halt and they could reunite with their sons and fathers. Climbing the gentle slope into town, the regiment was wheeled onto the green just north of the church, the exact spot Charles had departed from two years earlier. A halt was called. Bagley gave orders to Captain Young. He turned and faced the regiment.

"Take Care! Form columns into line, to your left, wheel!"

The men turned.

"Take your ease! The colonel wishes to address you before dismissing."

Bagley walked to the center of the line of the regiment and faced his men.

"Men, you are home. You have served your colonel well and shown that the soldiers of Massachusetts are and have always been ready to drive the enemy of God and our king from our lands. Some of you have served with me for two years now, others just for this campaign. Our job is not complete. We must think about the coming spring. I know it is a long time until then but you must dig deeply into your own soul. You must talk to your families and you must decide if you can march with me once again to form an army against our enemies. I am very proud of you and the work that you accomplished under adverse conditions in New York. Without your work, your families would not have been safe here in Amesbury or anywhere in our colony. I will leave you now to be with your families and loved ones, to pick up where you left off and to return to your work at your farms or at the wharfs. Mr. Remick and his assistant will be collecting your muskets, accouterments and uniforms at the church by companies.

"You are the heart of our world here in America. I salute you."

Bagley quickly brought the back of his right hand up to his tricorn into a salute.

Captain Young ordered, "Present your, Firelocks!" The men instantly brought their muskets into the position of honor.

"Captain, dismiss the men," ordered Bagley.

"Take care! By companies, report to the church and the Quarter Master. Gentlemen, you are, dismissed!" yelled Young.

One at a time, the companies formed up at the entrance to the church and handed in their gear. Some of the families darted into the ranks and embraced the soldiers. It did not take long and Charles and his company had handed their equipment in to the Quarter Master and were back out in front of the church. It took no time and Charles found his family. Meeting them on the cobblestone walk before the church, they all took turns with long welcoming embraces.

"My son, oh Charles, how I have prayed for your return," cried his mother and she buried her head in his shoulder.

Enoch slapped Charles on the back. "Good to have you home, Charles."

Charles reached out his hand to Enoch's. "It's wonderful to be home. You can only imagine," answered Charles.

"Son." His father took Charles in his arms and pulled him close. "You're finally home. Thank Jehovah!"

Charles took both his parents in his arms and hugged them. He kissed his mother to reassure her and a tear ran down his face. "I am home." He sighed and closed his eyes.

Opening his eyes again, Charles saw Mary and her mother. He let go of his parents and gave Sarah a quick hug. "I am so glad you are home, Charles," said Sarah.

Charles looked at Mary, he reached out his arms to her and took her in them and gave her a long kiss. "I have waited too long for this," whispered Charles in her ear. "Did you get my letters? I have yearned for the day I could hold you once more."

"It is going to be all right now Charles," she whispered back. She kissed his neck. "I am with you now. You can rest now and forget," she reassured.

The family wasted no time, climbed on to Caleb's wagon, and hurried home. All along the way, Charles sat between his mother and Mary. He had one arm around each and could not help holding them tight. Enoch was his usual chatterbox and kept all lively on the ride home. Caleb sat tall and proud as he reined the team of horses through town parading his son, home from the war.

When the family reached the house, Enoch took the team to the barn and saw to their care and the rest of the family entered the kitchen. It was warm and was drenched in the sweet aroma of his mother's cooking. Charles gasped as he saw the fire. He would finally be warm; it had been so long. He walked directly to the fire and placed fresh logs on the hot coals in the hearth. He sat down on the chair before it, slipped off his shoes, placed his feet close and bent over rubbing his hands over the flames. He sat back, put his feet up on a bench and sighed. "I can't believe I'm finally here. This feels so good."

Everyone looked at him and chuckled.

"Mary, Sarah, let's get a feast ready for this poor boy," said Margaret. "Charles, you are just skin and bones," she scolded her son.

The three tore into the job like they were making a dinner for a king. It was no time and they announced supper was finished.

"You come over here now and fill your belly. I imagine it has been a while," Margaret coaxed Charles. "You sit here by Mary and Enoch." Everyone took a seat at the long trestle table. "Caleb, would you say the blessing," asked Margaret.

They all bowed their heads.

"Lord Jehovah. I have prayed daily that You would return my son safe to me. I know You only borrowed him to do Your duty to fight Your enemies. We have waited so very long to be able to hold our son in our arms and to have him with us. We thank you Lord.

We have reaped a good harvest this fall and we now have most of it set aside for the long winter. We pray Lord that you will not bring too harsh a winter upon us. We continue to fetch enough wood for the cold months and hope that Your snows will wait another week or two. Lord, we thank You for Your blessings daily, we thank You for this food and we thank You for bringing our son back safely to us today. In Your name we pray to You, Amen."

The table was filled with foods that Charles had forgotten existed. He gorged himself; eating such a quantity of food, that no one in his family could fathom. After about an hour the family was done and Charles pushed his chair back from the table and put his hands on his stomach. The women began to clear the table. "I am so stuffed. Ladies, I have not eaten such a wonderful meal as this since I left for the war. I do not think I can budge. If I can, I would like one more sliver of that apple pie. I'll just sit here and eat it while you are retting up the kitchen," said Charles.

Once he had finished, Charles went into the great room and joined his father who was sitting in his chair smoking his pipe. "Sit and relax son," Caleb told Charles. "Enoch, fetch Charles my bottle and two mugs. You know where I keep it, in the blue cupboard in the kitchen." Enoch scampered out of the room.

"Son, it is truly wonderful that you are with us again. I was not sure until your last letter if you would sign on for another winter or not. Two years is enough, at least enough to go without any time home to speak of. Your mother and I are so proud of you," boasted Caleb.

"I know, Father. It has been a hard year. I know that you expected me to take care of William, but there was nothing I could do," apologized Charles.

"Say no more, Charles. We did not expect you to save him. He was a man and he thought he needed to fight for his honor just as you did. There is nothing you could have done and we know that. We just wish you did not have to be there alone when he passed. Your mother and I suffered with such a great loss of one of our sons. Your mother and I wept every night. I was sick with grief and your mother fell into a deep depression. We thought and prayed for weeks about it. Finally, after talking to the reverend about it one day, he made us understand that we still had two wonderful sons and that some day we would have grandchildren as well. It was God's will and that we should be honored that William chose to fight for his God. Let's not speak of it tonight," responded Caleb.

"The things that I have been through. I am so tired, Father."

"You must rest," stated Caleb.

Enoch came in with two partial mugs of rum for his father and Charles. Charles and his father just sat, sipped their drink and relaxed, staring at the warm fire. It was not long and Charles eyes began to flutter and close periodically. Charles was asleep when the ladies came into the great room.

"We should not keep him up. He needs some sleep desperately," said Margaret.

"Let's wake him and tell him we are going home so he can sleep and that we can see him in the morning," offered Sarah.

Caleb nudged Charles and his eyes opened but his body moved little. "Huh?"

"I would bet you have not had a good night's sleep in months, Charles Nurse. We are going home and let you get one tonight. Would you come over for lunch tomorrow?" asked Sarah.

Charles slowly rose from his chair. "That is an excellent idea," answered Charles. "You are right, it has been a very long time. Let me walk you out," offered Charles.

He walked Sarah and Mary out to the carriage that Enoch had hitched for them. Sarah climbed in and Charles reached to help Mary up. He gave her a kiss on the cheek and whispered in her ear, "Tomorrow, my dear. I will call tomorrow."

Sarah and Mary left the Nurse home's lane and headed toward Charles's house. Charles went back in his parent's house, said goodnight to his parents and Enoch, went directly upstairs, and crawled into the extra bed in Enoch's room. He was exhausted.

The next morning Charles awoke and shuffled down the stairs. Entering the kitchen, his head was filled with the aroma of his mother's homemade bread. The rest of the family had eaten and were off to work, so Martha made Charles a hearty breakfast and he ate to his heart's content. After his meal, he went out and strolled in the fields behind the house. He went to the barn, saddled his horse and road to his house to meet Sarah and Mary.

His house looked in good shape; they had been taking good care of it. Mary met him at the door and gave him a hug and kiss. "It is so wonderful to have you home," Mary exclaimed.

Sarah offered Charles a seat by the fire and the three sat and talked for about an hour. Then Sarah got up and made final preparations on their lunch. "Come and sit you two, lunch is ready," said Sarah. The three sat and enjoyed soup, bread, chicken and some beans.

"Even though I have not eaten much the last few months, I can not eat another morsel. I am stuffed," boasted Charles. "Mary would you take a walk with me?"

"Just let me ret the table and I would be pleased to take a walk," replied Mary in a flirting tone.

The two strolled down the road toward town. Within no time, they were at the wharf and they decided to stop in and say hello to Caleb and the others Charles used to work with.

Jonathan Gooding met Charles at the door. "It is great to see you Charles. I did not think we would see you so quickly. The Lowell brothers were just here; you just missed them. They were telling us about some of their adventures. They say that you had a dreadful summer campaign."

"Well, there were parts of it that were definitely things that I would choose not to remember, but I know how much it is needed for us to have troops in New York to make sure the enemy doesn't advance any farther," responded Charles.

"They told us that you were serving a lot with Captain Rogers and his rangers?" asked one of the other men in the shop.

"I did, and found that service to be one of the better experiences of the summer. He is a warrior, a man of the woods as well as a statesman," said Charles.

"Are you planning on enlisting in the rangers?" asked Jonathan.

"No, I chose to serve with them because the army seemed to have stagnated around their forts and it appeared that they would not drive north to attack the French. I felt that if we were only going to sit on our duffs at Fort Edward and Fort William Henry that I could do some service for my colony by bringing back reconnaissance and by attacking the French with Rogers and his smaller parties," explained Charles.

"Well, does that mean that you intend to enlist in Bagley's Regiment again next year?" asked another man from behind one of the boat hulls. As the man stood, Charles could see it was Samuel Greenleaf.

"Samuel, of all the damned men! You know first hand what we went through these past two campaigns. I cannot say at this time if I will enlist in any regiment. I do know though that we have a duty, a duty to our colony, our God, our families and ourselves to see to it that the enemy cannot bring the war to our colony. We have the honor that God has given us to see to it that the papists and their heathen cannot succeed in subduing our armies and destroy His chosen, here in Massachusetts-Bay. There must be men, good men, soldiers who are willing to leave their families and farms and march to war to see to the safety of the rest. However, that is a decision that I am not ready to make yet. Under no circumstance, does that mean that I intend to not serve, but only that I must do some serious thinking before I commit again. I see it as a man's duty to protect his family if called," stated Charles.

Charles and Mary talked to Caleb and a few others and were on their way. They stopped on their way back to the farm and sat for a few moments under some tall maples.

"Did you mean what you said back there Charles? Would you enlist again?" asked Mary in a worried tone.

He took her in his arms and looked into her eyes before answering her. "My dear, I have waited so long to be back in Amesbury, to see you again and to hold you and be comforted by you. I have seen hell again this year and done things that I can never tell you. I feel it only fair to tell you one thing though." He hesitated for a moment. "If it comes down to it that my colony calls for an army for next spring and if it meant that I could save my family from an unspeakable fate, from the hell of war, you know I would enlist in a moment's warning. It is a man's duty and honor to serve his country and protect his family. I would serve."

There was little conversation on their walk back the rest of the way to the farm. Once inside Sarah made some tea and a lighter conversation was enjoyed. Late in the afternoon, Mary walked Charles to the door and he rode off to his parent's farm. Mary knew the answer to her questions about Charles's enlisting next year, but she wanted to hear it from his own lips. He was a true man of honor, he knew that if he was needed he would not hesitate and Mary understood and admired him for it.

Within days, Charles had regained his strength and was visiting most of the people in town that he missed. Things were slipping back into the old ways for him and his family. One thing still was lacking in his life and he intended to do something about it.

Charles picked up Mary for a ride in the carriage one morning. They headed out on the road leading north of the town. It was a lovely day, sunny and clear. The winter birds were seen fluttering about and they stopped in a meadow about a mile down the road. A family of deer was grazing at the woods edge. Charles pulled the heavy lap blanket up high on them and they sat and talked. As they talked, Charles became serious.

"I have missed you more than you can imagine. Mary, without knowing you were waiting for me I almost turned mad. I have a little money set aside, the farm and house and a good job at the wharf that I can get back. My life is not complete, but I believe that you can help me make it so." He took her hand and looked at her, deep into her eyes and asked "Mary, will you marry me?"

"Oh yes! I have always known that we were meant to be together. I have so hoped for you to ask!" Tears began to flow as she answered him.

"I do not want to wait," said Charles. "Let's get married in two weeks!"

Mary threw her arms around his neck and they kissed more passionately than ever before. "Yes Charles, yes," she whispered. "If that is what you want."

That night they told Sarah and Charles's family. Everyone thought it was a good union. They wasted no time in making preparations. The church needed to be scheduled, Mary needed a dress, Charles needed to do some work on his house and of course Margaret and Sarah had to tell the entire world, at least it seemed that way.

Mary took her mother and Margaret to the general store to look for fabric for her dress. They had to begin immediately, as they had less than two weeks to prepare it. Caleb and Enoch helped Charles with his house. He wanted to put a lean-to on the back and expand the bedchamber and kitchen. Many of Charles's friends showed up for days to help work on the project. All was going according to plans. Just one day before the wedding, everything was complete.

That Saturday Charles awoke early. He started the fire in the kitchen and put on some water to boil. Once it was hot, he made himself some hot chocolate, stepped out in the garden, and stood by the back fence looking out over his father's fields. Snow was just beginning to cover most of the land and any plants left now were just tan and brown shafts poking through a carpet of snow white. Frost this morning clung to the bare branches of every tree. He sipped his drink and thought about his family, the life his grandparents had here settling the land, how his parents had prospered here, and glancing to the east, he could see the edges of his own property. He visualized his fields and his own children running through those fields enjoying their life, safe and secure. Before long, it was time for him to get ready.

Charles went inside and put on his best suit of clothes. He pulled on his white hose, navy woolen breeches, and buttoned up a brocade waistcoat. He tied his hair back in a navy hair ribbon and put on his navy coat. Enoch had hitched the family carriage and before long, they were all in it riding down the road to town. Charles was getting more nervous every step the horses took. They arrived at the church a few minutes early. It was not to be a very large wedding, family and about thirty friends. Some had arrived already and Charles and his family greeted others as they arrived. The Reverend Wells stood outside the church with Charles and Caleb shaking hands of those who arrived. It was not long before the church bells rang and Reverend Wells told Charles it was time for him to enter the church and take his spot up front.

In a few moments, Sarah entered the church. Then Charles glanced back at the church doors and Mary appeared. She was radiant! Never before had he feasted his eyes on such a vision of beauty. Her dark auburn hair was pulled back on the sides and was swept up and held in place with a ring of winter daisies. The rest of her hair brushed her shoulders in long ringlets. Her gown and bodice were cream silk brocaded with red and yellow flowers. Her petticoat was a pale yellow silk tabby weave that was quilted in a floral design. About her neck, Mary wore a simple charm on a yellow velvet ribbon. She carried a simple bouquet of dried baby's breath. As she began to walk down the aisle of the church everyone stood. Charles could feel his knees shake.

As Mary reached the front of the church, Charles put out his hand and took hers in his. The Reverend Wells welcomed everyone and then began to speak to Charles and Mary. The service was not long. Margaret could be heard periodically crying. Charles peeked over at his parents and saw his dad sitting, relaxed and proud of his son. Mary beamed with excitement and Charles's smile could not be wider.

"Charles Nurse. Do you take Mary Elizabeth, to be your lawfully wedded wife? To keep her and hold her, for richer or poorer, in sickness or in health, till death you do part?" spoke the reverend.

Charles said in a shaky voice, "I do."

Then the reverend spoke to Mary. "Mary Elizabeth. Do you take Charles as your husband, for richer or poorer, in sickness or in health, till death you do part?"

"I do," whispered Mary.

"Is there anyone here that knows why this man and woman should not be joined in marriage? Let him speak now, or forever hold your peace." The reverend paused. Then he went on. "Then, I now pronounce you, man and wife. You may kiss her, Charles."

Charles put his arms around Mary and they gave each other a kiss.

"Know that what God has united, may no man separate," stated Wells.

The reverend had Charles and Mary turn around and face the congregation and stated, "I now introduce to you, Mr. and Mrs. Charles Nurse.

With those words, Charles and Mary walked down the aisle and out the church doors. What a wonderful day it had been. All the friends and family crowded around the new couple congratulating them and telling them, what a wonderful life they were going to have. They were both elated.

The November wind blew softly into their faces. The chill let them know that things were changing in nature as well as in their lives. They were starting a new stage in their lives, a new life together, and a chance to leave part of the past behind them, to look to the future. They would now need to look toward their life here in Amesbury, starting a new family and setting forth the future for that family. Charles had dreamed of getting back to his family and Mary. He had arrived and made her his wife.

Charles picked Mary up by the waist and placed her in their carriage. They waved to the crowd and Charles snapped the reins. As the horse plodded forward, Charles put his arm around Mary and she nestled into his shoulder. A very light snow began to fall from the sky and as the gentle breeze tossed leaves on the road before their carriage. Charles began to think to himself. Now he must build a future for them and their children to grow up in. He also dreamed of having a country and colony where his children and his children's children could be who they wanted to be and do what they wanted to. Charles wanted a place where they could be freeborn Englishmen and free from the fear that the French could attack their settlements, their families, their way of life.

There would be hard choices to make to ensure their new family could build their dreams, but Charles knew they could make those choices together now. He would do everything in his power to grow, cherish and protect his family, even if that meant some day going back to the army. What would their future hold for them? Could they ever be rid of the fear of the French?